My Sister, My Slave

'Can I get you some cookies or anything?' Amanda said. 'A glass of milk?'

'I'll have some ice-cream,' I said.

Amanda smiled. 'Sure thing,' she said.

'And I'll have some milk and cookies too,' I said.

'Right!' Amanda vanished like an obedient genie.

Five minutes later she was back with a glass of milk, a bag of chocolate cookies and a dish of choc-choc chip ice-cream.

'I'll leave you alone then,' she said. 'If there's anything you need, just holler, right?'

Right! I thought. *Prepare to be hollered at, Amanda!*

My Sister, My Slave

Allan Frewin Jones

Series created by
Ben M. Baglio

RED FOX

A Red Fox Book

Published by Random House Children's Books
20 Vauxhall Bridge Road, London SW1V 2SA

A division of Random House UK Ltd
London Melbourne Sydney Auckland
Johannesburg and agencies throughout the world

Papers used by Random House UK Limited
are natural, recyclable products made from wood grown in
sustainable forests. The manufacturing processes conform to
the environmental regulations of the country of origin.

Set in 12/14 Plantin Roman by Intype, London

Printed and bound in Great Britain by
Cox & Wyman Ltd, Reading, Berkshire

RANDOM HOUSE UK Limited Reg. No. 954009

ISBN 0 09 938391 8

Chapter One

'My arm's getting stiff,' I told Amanda. 'Is there any chance of you finishing off in the next three months?'

I must have been lying there holding that apple for half the afternoon. I mean, I don't mind helping my sister out with her art projects, but there are limits to how long a person wants to sit clutching an apple and not daring to move while a person's older sister is drawing her.

'Five minutes, Stacy, and I'll be through,' Amanda said.

'You said that ten minutes ago,' I reminded her.

'You can't rush art,' Amanda said.

'You could kind of *nudge* it along though, couldn't you?' I said.

I'd only volunteered to be Amanda's sitter because Mom was having one of her crazy cleaning days down in the kitchen. Posing for

Amanda was a good way of getting out of being hauled off down there to help.

There were plenty of other things I could have been doing. For starters, I was a whole week behind in my diary entries. I could imagine today's entry: *Sunday. Broke the all-America apple-holding record, junior division.*

'I can't concentrate if you keep talking,' Amanda said, frowning at me over the drawing board she had propped up on her knees.

I sighed and wriggled myself into a more comfortable position on her bed.

'Don't move!' Amanda snapped. Amanda likes to snap. Maybe Mom watched a lot of programmes about alligators while she was carrying Amanda.

My sister says it's actually because she has an *artistic temperament.*

The Stacy Allen Dictionary
Artistic Temperament: A real good way for some people to get away with being snappy and bad-tempered.

'You're only drawing my *hand*,' I said. 'How long can that take?'

'I want to do it right,' Amanda said. 'It's very distracting the way you keep squirming around.'

'Sorr-ee,' I said. 'It's not like I'm getting

6

paid for this, you know. Some people might be grateful. Some people might think some kind of reward was called for.'

'No problem,' Amanda said. 'You get to eat the apple when I'm through, OK?'

'You're all heart,' I said. 'Did you know you wiggle your toes when you're drawing?'

You get to notice things like that when you've got nothing to do but stare into space for an hour.

I guess I should explain my sister a bit. She's thirteen. I'm ten, by the way, but she isn't three years older than me. It just looks that way right now because it was her thirteenth birthday recently and my eleventh birthday doesn't come for another five months. After that, she'll only be two years older than me. If you see what I mean.

You wouldn't think we were sisters, though, if you saw us walking down the street together. I take after my dad whereas Amanda's inherited her wavy blonde hair and her big blue eyes from Mom. What have I inherited? Crooked teeth and light brown hair that's so straight you'd think I went over it with an iron every morning before I hit the streets. Oh, yeah, I've inherited some real amusing freckles, too, and the kind of shape that you usually see in a *field* scaring crows off the crops.

I'd give you a big smile, but right now the brace on my teeth might dazzle you. I've got to wear it for two *years*!

It's a little too early to tell what my baby brother Sam's inherited from Mom and Dad. He's only thirteen months old. I've got big plans for Sam. I'm going to teach him everything I know. He's the sweetest baby in the whole wide world, and I'm going to be the best sister a kid brother could ever wish for.

Where was I? Oh, yes, explaining Amanda.

Easy, Step by Step Recipe for Making Your Own Amanda Allen

1. Take one cheerleader's outfit and place in a bowl.

2. Stir in some blonde hair, blue eyes, and a figure that's starting to get kind of curvy here and there. (But not as curvy as she'd like it to be.)

3. Add a whole bunch of dumb ideas about boys and trendy clothes.

4. Mix in three air-head friends called Cheryl, Rachel and Natalie.

5. Add a telephone to help with the hectic social life. (The entire recipe falls apart without a telephone.)

6. Season with a sprinkle or two of Genuine Artistic Ability.

7. Add a real superior attitude and mix well.

8. Place mixture in a house in Four Corners, Indiana.

Thirteen years later you'll have one Amanda Allen, AKA Bimbo Surprise!

What's the surprise? The surprise is that Amanda is a real good artist. *That's* how come I was posing for her with that apple. That's about the limit of my artistic ability. Amanda can just sit there with a bunch of pencils and a sketch pad and come up with the most life-like stuff you could imagine. I have trouble drawing a straight line with a ruler.

Right then, what Amanda wanted was a drawing of my hand holding an apple for a series of studies she was doing for school. I don't know what it was supposed to be called. *Hand with fruit*, I guess. You never get to see drawings of people with potato chips or hamburgers, do you? I guess there must be a reason for that. Maybe the people doing the posing can't resist eating them.

'Amanda, how much longer?' I asked after spending a few more minutes watching her toes wiggling away in her red socks.

Scribble, scribble, went her pencil. Wriggle, wriggle, went her toes. I really think that if you held Amanda's toes still, she wouldn't be able to draw a single line.

'Five minutes,' Amanda said. 'Now, keep *quiet*, will you?'

Five minutes. I think Amanda's watch must have been going *backwards*.

Out of the corner of my eye I spotted a little furry face looking around the edge of Amanda's bedroom door.

It was Benjamin. Benjamin is my cat. I got him as a Christmas present from Mom and Dad. Benjamin is a Russian Blue. A real pedigree cat. His fur isn't blue, though, it's grey. I guess the people who came up with all the cat names didn't think Russian Grey sounded as good as Russian Blue. And I read somewhere that they don't even come from Russia!

Now, if we had been in my room, Benjamin would have just marched straight in and up on to the bed. But Amanda doesn't like Benjamin coming into her room. It's not that she hates cats in general. It's just that Benjamin got in there a few times when he was a kitten and had a lot of fun knocking stuff off her shelves and chewing up her pencils and rolling all through her sketch pads and running off with her paintbrushes. You know, the kind of things any normal kitten would do.

The really big mistake he made was one

day when he jumped up on to the table while Amanda was mixing some paint. He landed with all four paws in the paint.

Amanda hollered at him, which was a real dumb thing to do, because it frightened the life out of him. He just ran for the hills. Well, for the catflap in the kitchen door, anyway.

I still don't see why *I* was the one who had to clean all the painty paw prints off Amanda's carpet. And off the hall carpet. And down the stair carpet. And across the living-room carpet and into the kitchen.

Because Benjamin was my cat, so Mom said, and I was responsible for him. But it was Amanda's paint. How come she wasn't responsible for *that*?

Benjamin slid into Amanda's room real quietly. She was too busy with her drawing to notice. I watched him out of the corner of my eye as he nosed around behind Amanda, sniffing all the interesting smells from the 'studio' half of her room.

One whole half of Amanda's room is full of her art stuff. A folder of drawings, a few mobiles and sculpture-things she's working on, and all the gear she needs to 'express' herself, as she says. And the wall over there is covered in watercolours and pencil sketches that she's done, as well as a few postcards and posters of work by her favourite artists.

Of course, it's easy to use half your bedroom as a studio if you have a room the size of Amanda's.

I watched Benjamin as he prowled around behind Amanda's back. Then he caught sight of her wiggling toes. Now if there's one thing Benjamin can't resist, it's wiggling toes. It's difficult to tell with Benjamin whether he knows it's just a foot in there, or whether he really thinks a wriggling sock is full of little creatures who want to be played with.

Either way, I could see what was coming. Benjamin's head went down, his front paws tucked under him, and his rear end shimmied from side to side as he prepared to pounce.

Pounce!

'Aieee!' Amanda screamed as Benjamin's claws and teeth sank into her foot and she jumped almost clear off the chair.

I burst out laughing.

The drawing board fell to the floor as Amanda hopped around the room holding her toes and yelling.

'You stupid *thing*!' she hollered.

'Don't talk to my cat like that,' I said. 'He's only playing.'

'I wasn't talking to the cat,' Amanda yelled.

'I was talking to *you*! You must have known he was going to bite me.'

'That wasn't a bite,' I told her as Benjamin came jumping up on to her bed to say hello to me. I gave his head a stroke. 'That was just playing, wasn't it, sweetie?'

'Get him off my bed!' Amanda yelled.

I sat up, picking Benjamin up. 'Love me, love my cat,' I said to her.

'That's just fine,' Amanda said. 'I hate both of you!'

'In that case,' I said, real dignified, 'this artist's model is quitting.' I took a bite out of the apple and got up off her bed. 'And next time you want someone to pose for you, try using a mirror. Although it'll probably *crack*!'

I walked out, carrying Benjamin in my arms.

'Good boy!' I told him out in the hallway. 'You get a special treat for that.'

We're quite a team, Benjamin and I.

We went downstairs and into the kitchen to find Benjamin something nice to eat. Oops. *Big* mistake. Chore alert!

Mom was in there in the middle of all her cleaning.

'Have you finished sitting for Amanda?' she asked.

13

'Yes,' I told her. 'I quit. She doesn't pay enough.'

'Good,' Mom said. 'So you're free to help me, huh?'

Heck! I walked straight into *that* one!

'I'd really like to,' I said. 'But I've got some homework to finish. I've got to hand it in tomorrow.'

'What homework?'

'Um, maths.' I said, thinking quick. 'Sorry, Mom. You know how it is, work before pleasure.'

'You can do it after dinner,' Mom said. 'Grab a cloth.'

'What about Amanda?' I said. 'I don't see why I should be the only one doing chores around here. Can I go and call her?'

'Yes,' Mom said. 'You do that.'

I yelled up the stairs, 'Amanda! Mom wants you! Come out, come out, wherever you are!'

'I'm taking a bubble bath,' Amanda hollered back.

Now this is a perfect example of how my sister manages to get out of chores around the house.

I ran upstairs. I could hear water running in the bathroom, and the smell of that strawberry bubble bath she uses in there was creeping out under the door.

'Mom wants you to help clean the kitchen,' I shouted, hammering on the door.

'Get lost,' Amanda yelled. 'I only just got in here.'

'You can't stay in there all day,' I said.

I heard her laughing over the noise of the water. 'Don't bet on it, kid,' she said.

I knew from experience what would happen. The moment Mom and I had finished in the kitchen, Amanda would appear at the door and say, 'OK, guys, what can I do to help?'

Chapter Two

'OK, guys,' Amanda said, appearing at the kitchen door almost an hour later. 'What can I do to help?'

Mom and I had gotten the whole kitchen cleaned before Amanda so much as showed her *nose* in there.

'Oh, gee,' she said, looking around. 'Are you done already?' Mom and I were at the table having a slice of cherry pie as a reward for all our hard work.

Amanda came over and just lifted my slice of pie off the plate and took a big bite.

'Will you quit that?' I said. I hate the way Amanda does that. 'Mom! Tell her!'

'There's plenty more in the fridge,' Mom said.

'That's OK,' Amanda said. 'I only wanted to try it out.' She gave me a big, cheesy grin as she put the remains of the slice of pie back on my plate. 'There you go, little sis, you get *all* the rest for yourself.'

'Was it nice?' I asked.

'Yup,' Amanda said, sucking her fingers.

'I thought so,' I said. 'Benjamin took a lick of it just before you came in, and he seemed to like it.'

Amanda made gagging noises and looked around for the cat to check whether I was telling the truth. Benjamin was over by the fridge grooming his whiskers.

'Mom! He didn't!' Amanda spluttered. 'That's so gross!'

'Calm down.' Mom said. 'She's only kidding you.'

'I hope your teeth rust, Stacy!' Amanda said.

'Cut that out, Amanda,' Mom said. She doesn't like it when Amanda makes fun of my brace. (And neither do I, for that matter!) 'If you're looking for chores,' Mom said, 'the bathroom needs cleaning.'

I could tell that Amanda was trying to think of an excuse to get out of it, when she was saved by the ringing of the telephone.

'That'll be for me,' Amanda said, disappearing out of the kitchen like she was attached by a wire to a taking-off jet plane.

'It might be your father,' Mom called. 'He said he'd call today to let us know when he can get down here.'

17

My dad is a travelling salesman. He works in the publishing industry, selling books to bookstores. Sometimes he has to be away from home for weeks at a time, but last time he called us he said he'd be getting a few days off soon. I was really looking forward to having him home for a while.

He's making less money these days, which is why Mom has had the basement converted into a home office. Mom works as a proof-reader for real dull academic books. Right now she's working on one called *Fourier Series and Partial Differential Equations*. I peeked at a page of it the other day. Sheesh! If boredom was rocket fuel, that book would get you to Mars.

Anyway, judging from the way Amanda was yakking on the phone, it must have been for her after all. One of her Bimbo friends.

My pals call Amanda and her bunch the Bimbo Brigade, because all they ever talk about is clothes and rock stars and whether their hair is styled the way they say it should be styled in those magazines they read.

Amanda and the Bimbos call me and my friends the Nerds. I don't know why. We're not in the least bit nerdy. I think they just like annoying us.

'Oh my gosh!' I heard Amanda yell. 'I forgot

all about it! No, pick me up here, will you? Give me half an hour.'

She slammed the phone down and gave a shriek.

'Amanda, honey, what's the problem?' Mom called.

Amanda was already halfway up the stairs, yelling something about a cheerleading practice.

Amanda is the head cheerleader at our school. She is *very* proud of that. You'd think she'd been made Commander-in-Chief of the *army* the way she behaves. She has a different cotton sweater from the other girls. She gets to make up new cheers for special occasions, and she gets to tell the squad what to do all the time. Talk about power!

'Panic stations,' Mom said. 'As usual.'

I wasn't so sure. I wouldn't put it past Amanda to have somehow *arranged* to get a phone call right then so she had an excuse for not cleaning the bathroom.

She came running down the stairs. 'Where's my cheerleading outfit?' she yelled.

'In the laundry,' Mom said. 'You didn't tell me you needed it today.'

'I do. I forgot.' Amanda wailed. 'That was Cheryl. We've got a special practice this afternoon. They're picking me up here in *half an hour*!'

'Then you'd better go and get it from the laundry basket,' Mom said.

Amanda let out a groan and dashed back upstairs. There are times when it's like sharing a house with a swarm of mad hornets. Hornets in boots.

From way upstairs we heard Sam let out one of his waking-up cries. Not even Sam could sleep with hurricane Amanda crashing around the house.

'Sam's awake!' Amanda yelled. 'Mom! Sam's up!'

'Should I go and get him?' I asked Mom.

'Yes, I guess you may as well,' Mom sighed. 'I'd been hoping he might sleep for a while longer. I've got work to do downstairs this afternoon.'

'You work, then.' I said generously. 'I'll look after him.' Actually, I wasn't being all *that* generous. I like looking after Sam. Besides which, if I was looking after Sam there was no fear of anyone suggesting I might like to clean the bathroom.

Sam's cries stopped the moment I stuck my head around my parents' bedroom door. He gave me a big smile. I picked him up, all warm from his crib, and carried him downstairs.

At the moment he's got very blue eyes and this soft fine blonde hair. He looks a bit like Grandpa Allen, to tell you the truth. But then sometimes he looks more like Mom. It's hard to tell with Sam *what* he's going to end up looking like.

I sat at the kitchen table with him in my lap and opened up one of his picture books.

Mom was just heading for her office in the basement when Amanda came back down carrying her cheerleader outfit.

'The skirt needs pressing,' she said to Mom.

'You know where the iron is,' Mom said.

'Aw – Mom!'

'Don't "aw – Mom" me,' Mom said. 'You're perfectly capable of doing your own ironing.'

'Not as good as you do it,' Amanda said with a hopeful smile.

'Then you could use the practice,' Mom said. 'I've got enough to do.' She went downstairs, leaving Amanda fuming in the living room.

You wouldn't believe the performance Amanda went through setting up the ironing board. It was like watching a comedy show.

'What are you laughing at?' Amanda snapped.

'You,' I said. 'You should be on television

with that act. "Amanda Allen and her Amazing Uncontrollable Ironing Board".'

'Oh, ha, ha, Stacy,' Amanda said, fighting to get the ironing board to stand up. 'You're just so funny.'

'Not half as funny as Amanda, huh?' I said to Sam.

Amanda stretched her skirt out and started attacking it with the iron. Our school cheerleader outfits are these bright blue sweaters with the school initials on the front, and a short, pleated red skirt.

'So what's with the big panic?' I asked.

'We're working on a special routine for the swim meet next Tuesday,' Amanda said. 'We're supposed to be making up a new cheer, and I forgot all about it.'

'If it's just a practice, why are you bothering to get dressed up?' I asked.

'Don't you know anything, Stacy?' Amanda said. 'I'm the captain of the cheerleaders. I have to set an example.'

'Some example Amanda's setting,' I said to Sam. 'An example of how to *forget* there's a practice in the first place.'

The swim meet was taking place at the local swimming pool. All the schools in Four Corners were going to be there, but the special thing about it was that the state champion high diver had been invited along. Nat Peder-son. An Olympic level diver. A real celebrity.

'What are you planning?' I asked Amanda. 'Synchronized underwater cheerleading?'

Amanda put the iron down and went into the start of a routine. 'N – A – T,' she chanted. 'P! E! D! E! R! S! Yeay!' It ended up with a leap into the air.

'His name's PedersON,' I said.

'I know,' Amanda said. 'We don't have it all worked out yet.'

The phone rang.

'That'll be for me.' Amanda said, dashing out.

'Amanda! The iron!' I yelled. She'd left the iron lying on her skirt.

I grabbed Sam and went to rescue her skirt.

'Mom!' Amanda hollered. 'It's for you!' I sat Sam down on the floor.

'Oh, thanks, Stacy.' Amanda said, coming back in and seeing the iron in my hand. 'Can you finish that for me while I look for my shoes?'

'Hey! Wait a minute!' But she was already out of there.

I looked down at Sam. 'Should I do this?' I asked him.

23

He clapped his hands together and gurgled happily.

'OK,' I said. 'If you say so. Just this once.' Sometimes it's easier just to go along with Amanda than to make a big thing out of it, and I didn't want Sam thinking I wasn't a nice person.

I'd just finished pressing her skirt when the front doorbell rang.

'Someone get that for me,' Amanda hollered from her room. 'It's Cheryl.'

Someone? For 'someone' read 'Stacy'.

I picked Sam up and went to answer the door.

'Hi, Sam. Hi, Stacy,' Cheryl said. 'Is Amanda ready?'

I think Cheryl Ruddick is the Bimbo that annoys me most. Did you notice how she said 'hi' to Sam *first*? If I answered the door with a doughnut in my hand she'd probably say, 'Hi, doughnut, hi, Stacy.' She's a *pain*. She's got this way of looking at me like I'm not really there. I'm sure a lot of Amanda's worst ideas come straight from Cheryl. Just for the record, she looks kind of like a hyena standing on its hind legs. A hyena with flowered pants and long brown hair that looks like it's been borrowed from a porcupine and fixed in place with glue.

'Is that you, Cheryl?' Amanda yelled down the stairs. 'I'm almost done. Stacy, have you finished ironing my skirt?'

Cheryl grinned from ear to ear. 'Amanda's little helper, huh?' she said, looking at me standing there holding Sam. 'You'll make someone a great little housewife one day.'

You know, there are times when I'd like to bite Cheryl Ruddick right on the nose!

There were a couple of frantic minutes while Amanda got all her stuff together.

'Hey,' I yelled. 'Aren't you going to put this ironing board away?'

'I don't have time,' Amanda shouted. 'You do it!'

'What am I,' I yelled as she went sweeping out the front door, 'the house *slave*?'

The last thing I heard as she slammed the door was a shriek of laughter from Cheryl.

'You know, Sam,' I said. 'Once, just *once*, I'd like to get Amanda running around after me for a change.'

I didn't realize it then, but I was about to have my wish come true. In a big way.

Chapter Three

'Hi! Stacy!' I looked around. It was Cindy. She waved and came running up the road.

Cindy Spiegel is my absolute best friend ever. I don't even mind that she's so pretty, and that she's got this wavy auburn hair that I'd kill for. I guess you kind of forgive your best friend for things like that.

Just recently I've been busy forgiving her for starting her growth spurt before me. She's two inches taller than me right now. If she keeps growing at this rate, I'm going to need a stepladder to *talk* to her.

I waited for her to catch up with me and we walked through the school gates together.

'Did you have a nice weekend?' she asked.

'Sure,' I said. 'My dad called Sunday night. He's going to be home for a few days next week.'

'Oh, that's great,' Cindy said. She knew how much I missed my dad. Our house always seemed much nicer when he was around. 'Will he be home for long?'

'For a whole week,' I said. 'He's coming down on Sunday, and he doesn't have to go back until the following weekend.'

'I bet your mom's looking forward to it,' Cindy said.

'No kidding,' I said. 'She's in a good mood already.' I grinned. 'Seven days of having Dad home should keep her in a good mood for the next month. She's always grouchier when he hasn't been home for a while.'

That was true although Mom always said it was Amanda and I who were the real grouches when Dad was away. Not true! Amanda might be a grouch, but not *me*.

We met up with Fern and Pippa in the corridor where we had our lockers. Fern Kipsak and Pippa Kane make up the rest of our gang. (The gang Amanda's Bimbo pals call the Nerds.)

Fern is the smallest of us, but she's also the loudest and the funniest. Pippa is the *brain*. She's your original absent-minded professor type. Really good if you need to know the capital of Peru, but a total dummy when it comes to anything practical.

We headed off to class. Cindy and I sit together, with Fern and Pippa behind. Sometimes we get separated when Fern cracks one of her jokes and we get the giggles, but normally we all hang out together.

Ms Fenwick, our teacher, had a special announcement. Ms Fenwick is pretty old, but she doesn't have any grey hair yet. Her hair is brown. She looks like an eagle, with this big hooked nose and piercing eyes that can see clear through your desk to check if you're reading a magazine.

'Listen up, class,' Ms Fenwick said. 'Now you all know about the swim meet next Tuesday, and that Nat Pederson will be coming along to show us some of the high diving that is going to win America a gold medal at the next Olympics. But what you may not know is that Nat is also very involved in SOC. Now, do any of you know what the acronym SOC stands for?'

'What's an acronym?' Fern hissed.

'It's when the first letters of the name of some group are run together to make another word,' Pippa whispered.

See what I mean about Pippa being the brainy one?

Ms Fenwick wrote SOC on the board. 'Anyone?' she asked.

Betsy-Jane Garside stuck her hand up.

Betsy-Jane is teacher's pet. I bet she *sleeps* with her hand up.

'Save Our Cetaceans,' Betsy-Jane sang, looking around to make sure no one had missed it.

'Correct,' Ms Fenwick said. She wrote it out in full on the board. 'And does anyone know what the word *cetacean* means?'

'Whales and dolphins and things like that,' Pippa said before Betsy-Jane had the chance to open her mouth.

'Well done, Pippa,' Ms Fenwick said. 'That's correct. Cetaceans are sea-going mammals. Many types of cetacean are on the endangered species list, and SOC is one of the groups who work to try and make sure that whales and dolphins and porpoises do not become extinct.'

I was all for that. I like whales. Especially humpbacks. It's difficult not to like something that goes around *singing* all the time. Considering the problems that we human beings give them, it's a wonder whales have got the *heart* to carry on singing.

'I thought it would be a nice gesture,' Ms Fenwick said, 'if we produced an exhibition about cetaceans. Something that we could set up at the swimming pool for Nat Pederson to see.'

We all thought this was a good idea. Ms Fenwick said we should form ourselves into small groups, and that each group should research a particular cetacean.

'Can we do humpback whales?' I asked real quick, before anyone else got there first. I'd seen a programme on television about hump-backed whales, so I already knew a little about them. I knew, for instance, that human beings were their only real enemy, and that they'd been hunted until there were hardly any left.

I knew how they must feel. Sometimes Amanda makes *me* feel like an endangered species.

The Stacy Allen Encyclopedia of Animals
Number 346: The Stacy Allen *A cheerful happy-go-lucky creature, driven to the edge of extinction by the Big-headed, Blonde-plumed Amanda. For more about the Amanda, see under the heading of "Monsters of the Deep".*

'OK, Stacy,' Ms Fenwick said. 'Your group can do a project on humpbacks. Now, what I'll do is write down all the different types of cetaceans, and we'll make sure everyone gets something to work on.'

The four of us looked around at one

another. No prizes for guessing who was going to be in *my* group.

After school that day the four of us headed for the town library to find ourselves some books on humpback whales. We'd decided that we were going to go all out to produce the best whale project in the class.

The main library in our town is a huge, modern glass and steel building with about a million books in it, all divided up into sections so you can find what you're looking for without too much trouble.

We got there just as Betsy-Jane Garside was walking out with a big pile of books under her arm. We might have known she'd get there first.

'The animal section is on the second floor, room 2B,' she told us.

'Have you *left* anything?' Cindy asked, looking at the way Betsy-Jane was struggling with her pile of books.

'First come, first served,' Betsy-Jane said, giving us one of her irritating smirks.

We watched her stagger down the steps then headed up to the second floor. The section on cetaceans looked like a mouth with half the teeth missing. Betsy-Jane had sure been busy there. All the best books were gone.

'Let's find one on breeding piranhas,' Fern

said. 'Maybe we could train a bunch of them to eat Betsy-Jane the next time she goes swimming.'

I liked *that* idea. I could see it now: Betsy-Jane does one of her show-off dives into the pool. There's this big rush of bubbles then chewing noises, and five minutes later, all that's left of Betsy-Jane is a heap of bones.

We managed to find a few books that Betsy-Jane hadn't whisked away. Most of them only had a small part about humpbacks, but there were a few really great pictures. One that I especially liked was of a whale coming right up out of the water, almost standing on its tail.

'We could do drawings,' Pippa suggested. 'That'd make our project really stand out.'

'Don't look at me,' I said. 'I can't draw to save my life.'

'Me neither,' Cindy said.

'Me neither, either,' Fern said.

'Amanda can,' Pippa said, looking at me. 'Your sister could do some really great drawings for us.' She flipped the pages of one of the books. 'Like *this* one.' It showed the triangular flukes of a whale slapping at the surface of the sea, sending up huge fountains of white water. 'Wouldn't that be great?'

'I'm not asking Amanda for any favours,' I

said. 'She never does anything without expecting something back.'

'I'm sure we could copy some pictures ourselves,' Fern said. 'It can't be that hard.'

We picked a few books and took them back
to my house for a better look at them.

I got some blank paper and tried copying
the picture of the splashing whale tail. We all
sat around to examine it. I sat on my heels,
chewing my pencil.

'What do you think?' I asked.

'It doesn't look like anything much,' Pippa
said.

'Oh, thanks,' I said. 'You do better.' But
she was right. I'd done my best to copy the
photograph, but somehow the sea didn't look
like sea and the tail could have been *anything*.

'How come your sister is so good at this
stuff and you're so hopeless?' Fern asked. Fern
has a habit of saying really blunt things like
that. She's not too aware of hurting people's
feelings.

'I told you I couldn't draw,' I said. I slung
the pencil at her. 'Let's see *you* produce a
masterpiece, then.'

Fern's attempt didn't look any better than
mine.

'What's *that*?' I asked, pointing to a bunch
of little 'm's Fern had drawn over the weird-

looking tail. (You wouldn't have known it was a tail at all – it looked more like the back end of a crashed airplane.)

'Seagulls,' Fern said. 'Don't you know seagulls when you see them?'

'Sure I do,' I said. 'And *those* don't look anything like seagulls. They don't look like *anything*.'

Fern looked at Cindy and Pippa. 'Come on, you guys,' she said. 'They're seagulls, aren't they? Can't you see?'

'Looks like a bunch of 'm's to me,' Pippa said. 'Where are their beaks? Where are their feet and everything?'

'They're seagulls off in the distance,' Fern said sulkily. 'Honestly, I give up with you guys.'

'Are you sure you don't want to ask Amanda to help us out?' Cindy said.

'I'll have a shot at it,' I said. 'But don't expect any miracles. She doesn't exactly fall over backwards to do me favours, you know.'

I left them looking through the books and went down the hall to Amanda's room.

Now, Amanda likes people to knock before they bust in on her. Most of the time I don't bother, but this time I thought a little diplomacy might be called for, so I tapped on her door and waited for her to say 'Enter.'

'What?' came this really irritated sounding voice.

I stuck my head around her door. She was sitting on her bed with her face in a book.

Shock! Amanda *never* reads books.

'Oh, sorry,' I said. 'I thought this was Amanda's room. I guess I got the wrong door.' Yeah, I know that wasn't a good way to start when I was after a *favour* from Amanda, but my mouth kind of runs away with me sometimes, and it really was a surprise to see her sitting there with a book.

'Yeah,' Amanda said. 'You got the wrong door the same place you got the wrong *face*.' She didn't sound like she was in the mood to be asked for help. 'What do you want?'

Be *nice*, I thought. *Show an interest*. 'What are you reading?'

'*Junk*,' Amanda said, 'Old Man Townes says I've got to do a report on it by next Wednesday. He's threatened to get me taken off the cheerleading squad if I fail English, so get lost.'

'Have I ever told you how much I admire the way you can draw?' I said brightly. 'I mean, you've got to be the best artist in Four Corners.' I gave her a big smile. 'Maybe in the whole *state*.'

Amanda gave me a suspicious look. 'Whatever it is you want,' she said, 'the answer is no.'

'What makes you think I want anything?' I said, acting real surprised.

'Don't you?'

'Well . . . now that you mention it, there *is* something,' I said. 'I wondered, seeing as you're such a brilliant artist and everything, whether you'd like to do some drawings of whales for a project I'm working on?'

'Not in a million, trillion years,' Amanda said.

'You don't have to come to a decision right away,' I said. 'Think about it.'

'You were right when you said you'd got the wrong door,' Amanda said, going back to the book. 'Shut it on your way out.'

'Look,' I said. 'We're going to be sisters all our lives. I don't want you looking back over your life in thirty years and feeling real guilty that you refused to help me when we were kids.'

'I'm not a kid,' Amanda said. 'You're the kid. Now get lost. I've got to read this pile of garbage.'

I shook my head. 'This could have been a real turning point in our relationship,' I said. 'I just want you to remember that when you're old and miserable and no one comes to visit you in your lonely shack on the outskirts of town.'

I shut the door just as the book came flying at my head.

'Any luck?' Cindy asked as I went back into my room.

'She won't do it,' I said.

I sat down on the floor with them and stared at the photographs of the whale's big triangular tail. I picked up the pencil again and got myself a clean sheet of paper.

'If Amanda can do it,' I said determinedly, 'then so can I. All I need is a little practice.'

'Yes,' Fern said. 'Like three years of practice. We've only got until next week.'

'That's plenty of time,' I told her. 'I'm going to get this right if it kills me.'

I started drawing.

I can be pretty determined once I've made my mind up. And right then, I was *absolutely* determined that we were going to have some drawings with our project. *Without* Amanda's help.

Chapter Four

My bedroom may be smaller than Amanda's, but it's a whole lot nicer. I've got posters on the walls of animals and some really spectacular scenery like the Grand Canyon. Mom and Dad allowed us to paint our rooms the way we wanted. Mine is this real cheerful yellow, because yellow is the happiest colour I know. Amanda says it might be like living inside a vat of lemon Jell-o, but who cares about *her* opinion?

I kept working on that drawing way into the evening. I only stopped for dinner, and I ate as quickly as I could so I could get right back up there.

The floor of my bedroom was covered in screwed-up sheets of paper. Cindy and the others had gone home by then, but I wasn't about to give up.

'Benjamin! Will you quit that?' I said for the hundredth time, as he sidled in between me and the paper. He almost stuck his tail right up my nose as he nudged at my hand. He wanted to be petted, and nothing was going to stop him.

'Miroo!' he said, staring straight at me. *Pet me!*

'You are the peskiest cat in the world,' I said, rubbing his face with both hands. He really likes to have his face and under his chin rubbed. I cupped my hands together and he pushed his nose through them with this really blissful expression.

'Now,' I said, picking him up and dumping him in my lap. 'You sit there like a good cat and let me get on with this.'

He curled up, purring away like an engine.

I was on about my thirtieth attempt by then. And suddenly it worked! Suddenly it really did look like a tail. It wasn't brilliant, I had to admit that, but at last I was getting somewhere. At least now it wouldn't need a label under it, saying: *This is the Back End of a Whale – Honest!*

I began to feel like a real artist as I pencilled in the foamy outlines of all the water the tail was throwing up. I was really proud of myself.

Half an hour later, the picture was finished. It had taken all evening, but it had been worth it.

I looked at the drawing, chewing at the end

of my pencil. *Not bad*, I thought. *Not bad at all*.

I tipped Benjamin out of my lap and took the drawing down to show Mom.

'Hey, now,' she said as I stood in front of her, holding the drawing carefully by my fingertips so I wouldn't get any smudges on it. 'That's wonderful, Stacy,' she said. 'You've done really well.'

'You can see what it's supposed to be, can't you?' I asked cautiously.

'Of course,' Mom said. 'A whale's flukes.'

I was just beginning to enjoy my Mom's praise when there was the sound of feet on the stairs and Amanda appeared.

'Look what Stacy did,' Mom said. 'You'd better watch out, Amanda. You're not the only artistic one in this family any more.'

Amanda hung over the back of the couch, her chin propped up in her hands. 'Are you sure you're holding it up the right way?' she said. 'What's it supposed to be?'

'It's a *whale*!' I said.

'Oh, sorry,' Amanda said. 'I thought it was a bunch of flowers in a vase.'

'Amanda!' Mom said. 'Cut that out. Stacy's worked really hard on this drawing. At least you could say something nice about it.'

'Honestly, I thought that black thing was a

vase,' Amanda said. 'And look – don't all those white squirly things look like flowers?'

'That's the sea!' I yelled. 'That's supposed to be all the water splashing up.' I looked at Mom. 'It doesn't look anything like flowers.'

'Of course it doesn't, honey,' Mom said. She frowned at Amanda. 'You can see perfectly well what it's supposed to be,' she said sternly. 'Don't make fun.'

Amanda grinned. 'OK,' she said. 'It's a whale. If you say so.'

'It's as good as anything you could do!' I said.

'Maybe with my eyes closed and my hands tied,' Amanda said.

I glared at her and stormed out. It *was* a good drawing. Amanda was just being nasty because I'd done it without her help.

As I went upstairs, I heard Mom say, 'That was unkind, Amanda. I want you to go and apologize.'

'Why? What did I *say*?'

As if she didn't know!

A minute later her head appeared around my bedroom door.

'Sorry for being nasty about your drawing,' she said. She didn't even pretend to sound like she meant it.

'No, you're not,' I said.

She shrugged. 'Mom said I had to apologize. So I've apologized. Anyway, I was wrong. It doesn't look like a vase of flowers. It looks like a rat that's been run over on the highway .'

* * *

I was in the living room later that same night, lying on the rug and watching TV, Mom was in the armchair working on her embroidery. She says it helps her relax. She's been doing it for the last two years. I guess she likes to relax very slowly. It's going to be a picture of a big green tree full of all kinds of animals. She'd finished about a quarter of it and every now and then she'd show me a new animal. Right then she was working on the face of a deer. Don't ask me what a deer was doing in a tree. I don't know. Maybe it was a special breed of tree deer. Anyhow, it was looking pretty good.

Amanda came down and sprawled out in front of the television. I was still mad at her because of what she'd said about my drawing. But I thought of a way of getting even with her.

'How's that book going, Amanda?' I asked. 'Have you done that *report* you were supposed to be writing?'

'Nope,' Amanda said.

'Didn't you say it had to be in my next week?' I asked her.

'Nope,' Amanda said, staring hard at the television.

'I'm sure that's what you told me,' I said. Amanda glared daggers at me.

'What book is this, honey?' Mom asked.

'Nothing much,' Amanda said, giving me a look like she wanted me to shrivel up and die right there on the rug.

'What's it called?' Mom asked.

'*The Incredible Journey*,' Amanda said. 'It should be called *The Incredibly* Boring *Journey*.'

'And when do you need to have the report done by?' Mom asked.

'Not for a long time,' Amanda said.

'When *exactly*?' Mom asked. Mom always has to bug Amanda about her homework. That was why I mentioned the book in the first place. I knew Mom would be on Amanda's tail about it.

'Not for a week or so,' Amanda said. 'Can we change the subject?'

Mom doesn't get put off that easily. 'What *day*?' she asked.

'A week from Wednesday, I think,' Amanda said.

'Then don't you think you ought to have read it by now?' Mom asked.

Amanda gave this big sigh. 'OK, OK,' she said. 'I'll go and read it *now*, OK? I'll go up to my room right now, even though I've got a really bad headache and I'm totally exhausted. I'll stay up all night reading it. And if I ruin my eyesight from overwork and have to wear special glasses for the rest of my life. I'll know who to thank.'

'Now just hold it right there,' Mom said. 'The day you get eyestrain from overwork, young lady, I'll eat this *couch*! I'm always hearing from your teachers about you handing in work late. It's got to *stop*, Amanda. You've got to start taking your schoolwork seriously.'

I could tell by the tone of Mom's voice that she was getting annoyed. If Amanda had any brains, she'd have kept quiet right then.

'I would,' Amanda said. 'If any of it was *worth* taking seriously.'

'OK,' Mom said. 'I'll give you something to take seriously. Amanda. If I hear one word from school about you handing in work late or goofing off when you should be paying attention, I'm going to have you taken off the cheerleading squad. Is *that* serious enough for you?'

Amanda's mouth fell open. 'You wouldn't,' she gasped. 'Mom – you *couldn't*!'

'Just watch me, Amanda,' Mom said. 'Being

on the cheerleading squad is a *privilege*. And privileges need to be earned.'

I just sat there staring at them. I hadn't expected Mom to get so mad. I wouldn't have mentioned that report if I'd known *this* was going to happen.

'But it's my whole *life*.' Amanda wailed. 'You can't *do* this to me. It's not . . . it's not *fair*!'

'You know what you've got to do,' Mom said sternly. 'Get that book read and get that report written. That's all I'm asking. It's for your own good, Amanda.'

Amanda didn't say another word. She just jumped up and ran upstairs.

Wow! When Mom gets mad she doesn't fool around. Amanda is pretty cool about threats from teachers (I guess you get used to them after the first few years), but when Mom threatens something, you can bet your life she means it.

Mom looked at me.

'Stacy? Have you gotten your things together for the morning?' she said.

This was Mom's way of levelling things out. I got up.

'I'll do it right now,' I said. I got out of there before Mom had a chance to say anything else. When my mother's in *that* kind of mood, the best thing is to steer well clear of her.

Amanda must have heard me go upstairs because I'd only been in my room for two minutes when she came in.

'Don't you knock?' I asked.

I expected her to explode in my face, but she just reached behind herself and knocked on the inside of my door. She looked really upset.

'Can I come in?' she asked miserably.

'It's not my fault you haven't read that book,' I said quickly. I thought she'd come in here to give me a hard time about mentioning that report in front of Mom.

She didn't. She just sighed and sat down on my bed.

'She can't take me off the cheerleading squad,' she said. 'I'd die.'

'So do the report,' I said. 'You've got plenty of time to finish it.'

Amanda shook her head. She seemed close to tears.

'You don't understand,' she said. 'It's worse than that.'

'So tell me,' I said. I was feeling kind of guilty for getting her into trouble with Mom. The least I could do was hear what Amanda had to say.

'I've got to do this other project on the Great Lakes,' Amanda said. 'How am I going to get everything done in time? If I work on that darned book I'm going to be late with the other work. And if I do *that*, I'm not going to have time to finish the book report. Either way, Mom's going to have me taken off the squad.'

'If you did your work when you were supposed to,' I said, 'you wouldn't get into these messes.'

'Oh, *thanks*, Stacy,' Amanda moaned. 'Big help.'

'What can I do about it?' I said. 'You heard what Mom said. And she wouldn't have gotten so mad in the first place if you hadn't talked back.'

'She wouldn't have *known* about it if you hadn't talked about it in front of her. It's all your fault!'

'It is not,' I said. 'You're always late with your homework!'

'But the *squad*!' Amanda groaned. 'I'll be taken off the squad, Stacy! Don't you realize how much that means to me?'

'Then I guess you'd better get to work,' I said.

'I can't do it *all*,' Amanda said. She gave me a hopeful smile. 'You like animals, don't you?' she said.

'I guess so,' I said suspiciously.

47

'Families are supposed to help each other out, right?' Amanda said. 'Like if you were in real, deep trouble, I'd help you out.'

'You would?' I said.

'Sure I would,' Amanda said. 'And I was thinking. Maybe I could do those drawings for you after all.'

'Don't bother,' I said. 'I'm going to do them myself.'

'But I could do better ones,' Amanda said. 'You know I could.'

'I don't care,' I said. 'I don't *want* you to do them. You had your chance, and you told me to get lost.'

'That's a shame,' Amanda said. 'I thought we could do each other a big favour.'

'Like what?' I asked.

'Wouldn't you like to read a book that was all about animals?' She brought her hand around from behind herself and waved her book at me. 'You'll enjoy it,' she said. 'It's just the sort of thing you'd like.'

'Oh, right,' I said. 'And then I write your report for you, is that it? Forget it, Amanda. I'll do my own drawings, and you can write your own report.'

'You were the one who got me into this mess,' Amanda said. 'At least you could help me out a little.'

She had a point. I'd only been teasing when I'd mentioned the book in front of Mom. I hadn't expected Mom to react so badly.

'I don't know,' I said.

'Pretty please?' Amanda said. 'I'm in big trouble otherwise.'

'This is all your own fault,' I said. 'Why should I bail you out?'

'I'll do anything you say,' Amanda said. 'You can't just sit back and let Mom have me taken off the cheerleading squad.'

'You'll do *anything*?' I said. I could see how this could work to my advantage if I was smart.

'Sure,' Amanda said. 'Anything.'

'OK,' I said. 'I'll think about it.'

'Stacy, you're terrific,' Amanda said.

'Hold on,' I said. 'I only said I'd think about it.'

'That's fine,' Amanda said. 'You let me know what you want me to do in exchange.' She sure left my room looking a whole lot brighter than she had when she'd come in there.

Meanwhile, I had some thinking to do. If I was going to do that report for Amanda, I wanted to make sure I got plenty in return.

After all, if things were the other way around, there was no way Amanda would help *me* out without some reward.

The question was: if I *did* decide to help her out, what kind of reward could I go for?

Chapter Five

'You should have agreed to do it right away.'
That was Fern's first comment the next day
at school when I told the guys about Amanda's
suggestion. 'You could have talked her into
doing a *dozen* drawings for us.'

'I don't want her doing any drawings,' I
said. 'I'm going to come up with something a
whole lot better than drawings. Anyway, forget
that for now, and take a look at this,' I said.
I'd brought my drawing in, carefully rolled
into a tube and secured with a rubber band. I
unrolled it for them to look at.

'Stacy, that's great,' Cindy said.

'It should be,' I said, smiling at them over
the top of the drawing. 'It took me all night.
Come on, you guys, do we need Amanda?'

'It's not bad,' Fern said, looking closely. She
grinned. 'It could use a few seagulls.'

'Are you going to be doing any more?' Pippa
asked. 'I mean, it's really good, Stacy, but—'

'But?' I said. 'But *what*?'

'Well,' Pippa said. 'You wouldn't actually know it was a humpback, would you? I mean, *tails* are all pretty much the same, aren't they? What our project could really use would be a drawing of an entire whale. So people can see what the whole thing looks like.'

'Why didn't you say that yesterday?' I asked, irritated. 'I thought you *liked* this picture?'

'I do,' Pippa said. 'It's just not very informative.' Pippa likes to use long words like 'informative'.

'She's right,' Cindy said. 'Now you've got the hang of it, you could do a couple more, couldn't you?'

'It took me *hours*,' I reminded them.

'I bet Amanda could do them a lot more quickly,' Fern said. 'I still say you should have made a deal with her. After all, how long would it take you to read a book?'

'Will you shut up about Amanda?' I said. 'I'm not making a deal that involves her doing something she *likes*, while I slave over her report. She'd be laughing her head off at me.'

'So what are you planning?' Fern asked. 'If she's so desperate for you to do that report, you ought to make the most of it. Get her doing something for you that she *doesn't* like.'

'Exactly,' I said. 'That's exactly what I'm trying to come up with.'

'You should get her to pay you,' Pippa said.

'She should do some chores for you, at least,' Cindy added. 'When I help my brothers out, they do my housework for me.'

'Get her slaving for you,' Fern said. 'That's what I'd do.'

Amanda the slave? Would she go for that? Was she *that* desperate to get out of writing that report?

It wasn't exactly unusual for Amanda to let her schoolwork pile up on her. The Great Lakes project she'd told me about was probably already overdue. So now she only had time for *either* the project or the book report. But not both. It seemed a shame not to make the most of a situation like that.

I was pretty sure that if I came right out and said, 'Amanda, I'll do that report if you'll be my slave for the next week', that Amanda would tell me to get lost. But I could ask her to do a few small chores for me to start off with. And then I could sort of *build* it up, chore by chore.

I explained this idea to the others. 'She won't be able to say no,' I told them. 'Get it? Right up until the time I hand over the finished report, she'll have to do anything I tell her.'

'Snea-kee!' Fern said.

I can be sneaky when I want to. *Very* sneaky.

53

★ ★ ★

I finally caught up with Amanda at lunch break. She was with a bunch of the cheerleaders. They were practising the new cheer for Nat Pederson.

I watched them for a minute.

'OK,' Amanda said, pushing her hair out of her eyes. 'Let's try this *once* more.' She knelt. 'We start like *this*, right?' She bounced up, stretching her arms out to the left. 'N!' She swung her arms to the right. 'A!' Her arms went into the air above her head. 'T!'

'You did that the other way around last time,' Rachel Goldstein said. She's another of the Bimbo Brigade. All three of the Bimbos are on the cheerleading squad. Rachel has a face like a monkey, and these long, skinny arms and legs. She's also got bright carrot-coloured hair. I have nothing against carrot-coloured hair. It must be great for Halloween, or a costume party, but I wouldn't want to go around with a big bunch of wiry carroty hair all the time.

'No I didn't,' Amanda said.

'Yes you did.' Rachel said. 'You went like – kneel, jump, arms right *first*.'

'That's because I was *facing* you,' Amanda yelled. 'I was showing you which way *you* were supposed to go with your arms. I did it backwards on *purpose*. *Now* I'm doing it the right way.'

'I don't get it,' said another girl. 'Is the ' "N" to the right or the left, then?'

'Left!' Amanda howled.

'Your left, or ours?' Rachel asked.

'Aarrgh!' Amanda hollered, spinning around so she had her back to them. ' "N!" Arms *left*. "A!" Arms *right*. "T!" Arms above your heads. Got it?' She spotted me watching them and gave me a nasty glare. 'What do *you* want? This is private.'

I had my lips tight together to keep myself from laughing. 'Can I have a word with you?' I asked.

'Not now,' Amanda said. 'Can't you see I'm busy?'

'It's about that report of yours.' I said. 'That *thing* we were talking about last night?'

'Oh.' She looked around at the others. 'You guys keep on practising. I'll be back in a minute.'

She walked over to me, her face red from all the jumping she'd been doing. Over her shoulder I could see the other girls bouncing about like a bunch of Mexican jumping beans.

'So?' she said. 'Are you going to help me out?'

'I think we can come to *terms*,' I said.

Amanda beamed at me. 'Thanks, Stacy,' she said. 'You're a real pal.'

'Wait a minute,' I said. 'You haven't heard what I want in return.'

'OK,' Amanda said. 'How many drawings?'

'No drawings at all,' I said. 'That's not the deal. I want you to do all my chores for two whole days.'

Amanda frowned. I could see she was thinking about this, trying to figure out how much work it would involve.

'Two days?' she said. 'And then I get my report?'

'That's it,' I said.

She grinned. 'Deal!' she said. 'I'll let you have the book at the end of lunch break, OK?'

'Fine,' I said. 'See you later.'

Two days. Ha! She thought I meant the *next* two days. But that's not what I'd said. I'd said two *whole* days. Forty-eight hours. Forty-eight *solid* hours of chores. If she did one hour of chores a day for me, it'd still take her until the middle of next month to make up forty-eight hours.

That's what's known as outsmarting someone.

Chapter Six

I spent some free time during the afternoon reading Amanda's book. I was doing pretty well with it, and it wasn't a bunch of garbage at all. I could see why it was called *The Incredible Journey*. It was set in Canada, and it was about these three pets who get separated from their owners and who travel 250 miles through the wilderness to find them. A labrador, a bull terrier, and a Siamese cat called Tao. I liked the cat best of all.

It was really great, and as soon as I got home that afternoon I went right to my room and stretched out on the bed to read.

Benjamin curled up on my legs for a nap. 'Would you travel 250 miles to find me, huh?' I asked him, stroking his head. 'Would you fight porcupines and lions and grizzly bears?'

Benjamin started purring. That was his way of saying, *of course I would*.

A little later, Amanda stuck her head around my door.

'How's it going?' she asked.

'Fine,' I said. I was making a few notes as I went along and I had a page full of scribbles already. Once I'd finished the book, I didn't think it would take me more than a couple of hours to whip out a report.

'Can I get you some cookies or anything?' Amanda said. 'A glass of milk?'

'I'll have some ice-cream,' I said.

Amanda smiled. 'Sure thing,' she said.

'And I'll have some milk and cookies too,' I said.

'Right!' Amanda vanished like an obedient genie.

Five minutes later she was back with a glass of milk, a bag of chocolate cookies and a dish of choc-choc chip ice-cream.

'I'll leave you alone, then,' she said. 'If there's anything you need, just holler, right?'

Right! I thought. *Prepare to be hollered at, Amanda.* If she thought a snack counted as *chores*, she was in for a big surprise.

A little later I heard Mom's voice from downstairs. I didn't hear what she said, but I could tell from the tone that something was up.

I lifted Benjamin off my legs and went to my bedroom door to listen.

'I promised them I'd be there,' I heard

Amanda say. 'We've got to practise, Mom. I'm trying to teach them a new cheer, and it's taking for ever to get it in their heads.'

'And what about that book report of yours?' Mom said. 'How's that coming along?'

'It's all under control,' Amanda said. 'No problem.'

'Have you *done* it, Amanda? That's what I'm asking,' Mom said sternly. 'Your schoolwork takes priority over cheerleading practice, you know that.'

'I've started it,' Amanda said.

'Show me what you've done,' Mom said. Oops! When Mom's in *that* kind of mood, there's no getting past her.

'I left it at school,' Amanda said.

'I see,' Mom said. 'Then I want to see it tomorrow afternoon, Amanda. And if it's not darned near finished, you're going to be grounded for the rest of the week. Got me?'

Phew! I thought. It's a good thing Mom didn't know about Amanda's *other* project!

'Don't you trust me?' Amanda said in her hurt voice.

'Sure I trust you,' Mom said. 'About *this* much.' I could imagine Mom standing there with her fingertips an inch apart.

'Can I go now?' Amanda asked.

'I want you back here by eight,' Mom said. 'And no excuses.'

Amanda came thundering up the stairs and burst into my room.

'Stacy . . .?'

'I heard,' I said.

'What am I going to do?' Amanda asked in a panic. 'Mom wants to see what I've done.'

'Take these,' I said, handing her my notes. 'You'll have to copy them in your own handwriting.'

She grabbed the paper. 'Thanks, Stacy.'

'What about my chores?' I asked.

'I'll *do* them, honest,' Amanda said. 'Just make a list.'

You're probably thinking I was crazy to hand that stuff over to Amanda, but it only covered the first third of the book. I sure wasn't going to let her have any more of my notes until I got some work out of her.

Meanwhile, I put the book to one side and started on a good, long list of chores.

Amanda's Chores
1. *Getting stuff for me.* (Not just snacks, but *anything* I want. Even it if means her going out to the store.)
2. *Vacuuming my room and cleaning up after me.*

3. *Feeding Benjamin and checking him for fleas.*
4. *Taking the garbage out when it's my turn.*
5. *Washing the dishes when it's my turn.*
6. *Carrying my school books.* (That will *really* get to her! Especially if any of her Bimbo friends see it.)
7. *Shining my shoes.*
8. *Cleaning up after me in the bathroom.*

And that was just the stuff I could come up with in a few minutes.

I stroked Benjamin. 'We're going to enjoy this, aren't we, boy?' I said. 'We're going to enjoy this a *lot*!'

* * *

I didn't see much of Amanda for the rest of that evening. It was pretty clear that she was avoiding me as much as she could. She was probably hoping that if she kept out of my way for the next two days, I'd end up handing over the book report without her having done anything. Was *she* in for a surprise!

Still, she couldn't avoid me the next morning when I asked her to carry my bag.

'I've made that list,' I said as we walked in through the school gates.

'Great,' Amanda said in a really uninterested voice.

'Wait a second and I'll show it to you.'

I spotted Natalie heading toward us. Natalie is the third member of Amanda's Bimbo Brigade. She's the most stuck-up of them all. She's got the longest hair in the entire school. I mean, she *sits* on it. It's ash blonde and she's always playing with it and telling everyone how she has to brush it *one hundred times* before she goes to bed at night. Which sounds like a complete waste of time because underneath that hair she's got a face like a really surprised-looking gerbil.

'Hi, Amanda,' Natalie squeaked in that high-pitched voice of hers. 'You'll never guess who *I* met yesterday afternoon. Karen Masterson!' Her eyes grew wide. 'You know – Greg's sister.'

'Really?' Amanda said. 'Did you say anything?' She looked at me. 'Oh, I'll see you later, Stacy.'

'You can give me my bag back now,' I said.

Natalie gave her a puzzled look. 'Why are you carrying her bag, Amanda?'

'No reason,' Amanda said quickly, shoving my bag into my hands.

'What about that *list*?' I said.

'Later,' Amanda said, tossing her hair. I've

got this fantasy that one day she's going to do that and all her hair will come flying off like a wig.

'When?' I demanded.

'Soon. OK?'

They walked off. The last thing I heard Amanda say was: 'Did you ask her about Greg?' in a really excited voice.

I didn't know who Greg was, but I could tell from the tone of Amanda's voice that he must be someone she was interested in. Yuck! She gives me the creeps the way she goes on about boys.

* * *

I didn't manage to catch up with Amanda until after school. For someone who likes to be the centre of attention all the time, she's sure good at hiding when she wants to.

I got home before her and I was sitting on the couch in the living room, just about to finish *The Incredible Journey*, when Mom came up from her office with Sam in her arms.

'What are you reading?' Mom asked, sitting down beside me with Sam in her lap. 'Anything nice?'

'Yes,' I said, trying to keep the cover of the book out of sight.

Mom is always telling us that we should

help each other, but I was pretty sure that didn't include making deals that meant I did an entire book report for Amanda. Mom wouldn't approve of that at all.

She reached out and tipped the book up so she could see the title. 'Isn't that Amanda's book?' she said.

'Yes,' I said, trying to sound as innocent as possible. 'She lent it to me after she finished it. It's really good. You should read it, Mom.'

'I wish I had the time,' Mom said. She looked down at Sam, who was fast asleep. 'Will you keep an eye on your brother while I go and fix dinner?'

'Sure,' I said, as she carefully rested Sam on the cushions. 'What time on Sunday will Dad be home?' I asked.

'About mid-afternoon,' Mom said.

'Will he take us out?' I asked. I always loved it when we went on family trips in the car.

'Give the poor man a chance, honey,' Mom said. 'He'll probably be exhausted. How are you doing with your drawings? Have you done any more yet?'

'Not yet,' I said. 'We've got until Tuesday to finish the project.' A thought struck me. 'Will you and Dad be able to come over to the swimming pool on Tuesday? You'll be able to see our project there. It'll be on display.'

'We'll be there,' Mom said. 'Amanda's already asked. She wants us there to see the new cheer she's worked out to welcome Nat Pederson. We'll be able to see your display at the same time.'

Trust Amanda to get in first!

'Oh, and Stacy,' Mom said. 'I think you'd better do something about your room tonight. I've never seen such a mess.'

That was Amanda's fault. I hadn't cleaned anything up in there for a couple of days. *Well*, I'd thought, *if you've got a slave, you should give them plenty to do.* I hadn't counted on Amanda being so good at avoiding me.

★　★　★

'OK, Amanda,' Mom said as we sat down to dinner. 'Surprise me. Tell me you forgot to bring that book report home.'

'Not at all,' Amanda said. (Toss that hair, Amanda! Yeah! There she goes!) She took out my notes that she'd copied and laid them on the kitchen table in front of Mom. 'See?' Amanda said. 'All I've got to do now is write my report and it's all done.'

Sam tried to grab the paper and Mom had to lift it out of his reach real fast. The entire time she was reading it, Sam made his gimme-gimme noises and squirmed on her lap to get the paper and stuff it into his mouth. (He stuffs everything into his mouth. I'm sure glad people grow out of that. It would be weird, wouldn't it? Like, you're sitting at your desk in class. The teacher passes out the test, and the first thing everyone does is shove them in their mouths to see what they taste like.)

'Well?' Amanda said. 'Are you going to apologize for not believing I'd done it?'

Mom smiled and handed Amanda the notes. 'I apologize,' she said. 'It looks good. It shows you can do it when you try, Amanda.' She gave a small frown. She looked at me. 'Did you help Amanda with this at all, Stacy?'

Help! *Think quick, Stacy!*

'I haven't worked with Amanda on it at all,' I said. Well, that was true. I hadn't worked *with* her. I'd been doing the whole thing myself.

'Then I'm pleased with you, Amanda,' Mom said. I felt a twinge of annoyance. That was *my* praise Amanda was getting.

'Does that mean I get to stay on the squad?' Amanda asked. I could see what she was thinking. Half a report was better than no report at all. And if Mom lifted the threat of taking her off the squad, I could kiss my slave goodbye.

'You finish it first,' Mom said.

'Aw, but *Mom!*' *Amanda pleaded. 'You can see how hard I've been working on it.*'

'*Bring it to me when it's finished.*' Mom said firmly. 'I know you too well, Amanda. If I let you off now you'll just fall back into your old ways.' (Gee! Mom knows Amanda as well as I do!)

'OK,' Amanda said. 'But can I go see Cheryl now, like you said?' Amanda asked.

'I guess you can,' said Mom.

I didn't get a chance to corner Amanda for a little while. In fact, she was just heading for the front door when I finally caught up with her.

'Where are you going?' I asked.

'Cheerleading practice,' Amanda said.

'What about my chores?' I asked.

'Will you give me a break about those chores?' Amanda hissed. 'I'll start them as soon as I get back. Anyone would think you didn't trust me.'

'They'd be right.' I said. 'I don't.'

Amanda made shushing gestures with her hands. 'Keep it down, Stacy. You don't want Mom hearing. I'll see you later.'

And off she went. Harry Houdini should

take lessons from my sister, the way she gets our of things.

Introducing the Great Amanda Houdini – Escape Artist Extraordinaire! See her get out of doing a book report! Marvel as she escapes from the house instead of doing Stacy's chores! Gasp in wonder as she comes up with another excuse!

Yup, that's my sister, OK.

Chapter Seven

I finished reading Amanda's book that night. It didn't actually take me as long as I'd thought to write the report. I guess it's because I liked the book so much. I don't mean I want to dedicate my whole life to writing book reports, but it doesn't give me the shivers like it does Amanda.

I was waiting for her when she got home. I was standing at the top of the stairs with the list of chores.

Her face dropped when she saw me there.

'I need a shower,' she said, pushing past me. I left the list folded on the desk in her room.

I watched TV with Mom for a while then went back upstairs to check on Amanda.

She was in her room, lying on the bed listening to some music on her headphones with her eyes shut. The list was still folded on her desk. She hadn't even looked at it.

I crept over to the bed and turned the

volume up on her CD player. Amanda got up off the bed like she'd had an electric shock.

'Waahoop!' she yelled, ripping the headphones off. 'Stacy! What did you do that for?'

'Are you going to do those chores for me, or what?' I demanded.

'Not right now,' Amanda said. 'I'm exhausted. I've been jumping around all evening. I need a rest.' She sat up squirming her fingers into her ears. 'I'm sick of you whining about those chores, Stacy.'

'You promised,' I said.

'Look, Stacy, I know I promised. I'm not trying to get out of it. Honest.'

'So you can start by cleaning my room,' I said. I didn't mention that I'd deliberately let it get into a real mess for her. 'Mom wants it cleaned up right now.'

'Have you done the report yet?' Amanda asked.

'I've done most of it,' I told her. 'But you're not seeing another *word* until you start keeping your side of the bargain.'

'Tell you what, Stacy,' Amanda said. 'I'll do everything you want this weekend. How's that?'

'That's too late,' I said. 'Anyway, you'll just come up with another bunch of excuses.'

70

'Saturday,' Amanda said. 'That's my best offer.'

I glared at her. 'I know you, You have no intention of doing anything.' I was really mad at her now, especially since this meant I'd be spending the rest of the evening tidying my room so I didn't get into trouble with Mom. 'Well, Amanda Allen, you can do your *own* report!' I spotted the report notes on her desk. Before she could move, I grabbed the sheets of paper and ran out of her room.

I was standing in my room with the paper scrunched up in my hands when Amanda came running in.

'Don't be like this, Stacy,' Amanda said. 'I'll do your room. I'll do it right now, OK?'

'Forget it,' I said. 'Just forget all about it. I'll do it myself. And you can do that report on your own!'

Amanda gave me a weak smile. 'Aw, hey, Stacy, that's just silly,' she said. 'You've already done most of it.' She bent down and picked up some clothes off the floor. 'See?' she said. 'I'm picking up for you. Just like you asked.'

I sat on the bed. 'I want it done properly,' I said.

'Sure thing,' Amanda said. 'Anything you say. You're the boss.'

I gave her a big smile. 'That's right,' I said. 'I'm the boss.'

★ ★ ★

I was sitting on my bed playing tag with Benjamin with a red ribbon.

The Labours of Amanda Allen were well under way. She'd picked up all my clothes and taken the dirty ones to the laundry basket. Then she'd hung the rest in my closet before getting to all the *other* stuff I'd left all over the floor.

She looked at me. 'How's that?' she said. 'Clean enough for you?'

'What about my desk?' I said.

She gave a snort of annoyance.

'I want all the drawers sorted out too,' I said. 'And then you can sort my books in alphabetical order,' I added, nodding over to my shelves.

She stared at me for a moment as if she was about to tell me to get lost.

'No work, no report,' I reminded her.

Amanda got to work without another word. Not that I couldn't see what she'd have *liked* to have said.

She finished my desk while I continued playing tag with Benjamin. Then she started on my books. I'd been meaning to get my bookshelves in some kind of order for ages. I knew it really taxed her brain, and it would probably have taken me half the time, but, hey, if you've got a slave, you may as well give her plenty to do.

Amanda was in the middle of this when Mom opened my door and looked in.

'Isn't it time you girls were thinking about bed?' she asked.

'I'm almost done,' Amanda said.

Mom gave her a puzzled look. 'What's going on?' she asked.

'I'm just sorting Stacy's books for her,' Amanda said.

'I can see what you're doing, Amanda,' Mom said. 'The question is: why?'

Amanda shrugged. 'Why not? You're always telling us to help each other out. So I'm help-ing.' She gave Mom an uneasy smile. 'Sheesh!' she said. 'Some people are never satisfied.'

Mom gave her a suspicious look. 'I think Stacy can sort her own things,' she said. 'If you're looking for things to organize, Amanda, I suggest you take a look at your own room first.'

'OK,' Amanda said meekly. 'I'm done here, anyway. OK, Stacy?'

I looked around at my neat new book-shelves. 'Yes,' I said. 'That's fine. Thanks.'

'Hold it right there,' Mom said as Amanda headed for the door. 'What's the deal here? What have you two been cooking up?'

'Nothing,' we both said together.

'Hmmm,' Mom said.

Amanda gave her a bright smile. 'It's "Be Nice to Younger Sisters Week",' she said. 'Haven't you read about it in the newspapers?'

'Well, I'm glad to see it,' Mom said. But she didn't sound glad. She sounded real suspicious.

'It's a pretty sad world,' I said, 'if a girl can't help her sister out every now and then.' I gave Mom a big smile. 'Wouldn't you say?'

Mom left us with another really big 'HMMMM!'

My mother is the most suspicious person in the world.

'Do I get my report now?' Amanda said.

'You're kidding?' I said. 'We agreed two days, not one evening.'

'That's right,' Amanda said. 'Two days. Yesterday and today. So I'm done, right?'

I thought it was about time I let Amanda in on what I had really meant by two days.

She stared at me in disbelief as I explained.

'Forty-eight *hours?*' she said. 'No way!'

'You've just broken the deal, Amanda,' I said. 'Wave goodbye to your cheerleading.

I guess you'll get used to watching from the sidelines – *eventually!*'

'Why, you little . . .' Her voice trailed off. She took a deep breath. 'OK,' she said. 'You can have your forty-eight hours, Stacy. When do I get my report?'

I knew exactly what was going through her mind. She'd agree to *anything* to get her hands on that report. If I asked her to give me a piggy-back ride to California she'd have said yes. And the moment she had the report in her clutches, she'd back out of the whole thing, promise or no promise.

'I'll let you have it on Monday,' I said. 'That'll give you plenty of time to write it in your own handwriting.'

And, I didn't need to add, it meant Amanda would be stuck as my obedient slave for the next five days!

I was planning on taking full advantage of those five days. Cleaning up my room was just the start of it.

* * *

The next morning Amanda was about to go into the bathroom when I caught her.

'Me first, I think,' I said.

'What?' Amanda snapped.

'Don't forget the repor-ort,' I said in a singsong voice. 'Remember, it's "Be Nice to Younger Sisters Week".'

'Oh, yeah. Fine,' Amanda said, traipsing back to her room. Whoo! Power! We usually have fights over the bathroom in the morning.

'Oh, and I'd like to borrow your CD player, if that's OK,' I said.

Amanda gave me the sort of smile you see on the faces of dead fish. 'Sure thing,' she said. 'I'll go get it.'

She was going to lend me her CD player! She never usually let me within twenty feet of her CD player. In the past she's threatened to cut my hands off and stuff them down my throat, if I so much as *touched* her CD player.

Amanda carried my school bag to the bus stop that morning. I couldn't wait to get to school and give the guys an update on things.

When I'd told them about the deal I'd made with Amanda, they'd all said that she would find some way of worming out of her side of the bargain. Today, I was going to show them they were wrong.

Cindy and Pippa were standing chatting at the school entrance when Amanda and I arrived.

'See you later,' Amanda said.

'Hey, just a minute,' I said to her. 'Could you go put my stuff in my locker?'

Amanda gave a feeble smile and marched off with my bag over her shoulder.

We met up with Fern and I told them about how Amanda had meekly cleaned up my room the night before.

'You'd better make the most of it,' Pippa said. 'You'll see, the moment she gets her hands on that report, you're going to be looking for a new slave.'

'I know *that*,' I said. 'But that won't be until Monday, and in the meantime I'm going to have her running around after me until her legs wear down to her knees!'

'Way to go, Stacy!' Fern said. 'What sort of things are you planning?'

'You'll see,' I told them. 'Just make sure you're all in the cafeteria at lunchtime.'

★   ★   ★

It was the usual chaos in the cafeteria. Everyone shoving and pushing to get into line or to their favourite tables, all talking at full volume.

'Wait,' I told Cindy and the others as they headed for the end of the line. 'I don't see why we should have to bother with all this.'

'I'm starved,' Cindy said. 'All the best stuff will be gone if we stand around here.'

'Give me your orders and your money,' I said. 'We're having waitress service today.'

I nodded over to where Amanda and a few of her friends were waiting in line. 'You go get a table. I'll be over in a minute,' I told them.

They made their way through the tables to our favourite spot over by the windows. I could tell they were watching as I went up to Amanda.

'Hey, Amanda,' I said.

She stopped talking to Natalie and Cheryl and looked around.

'Oh, hi, Stacy,' she said.

'No butting in,' Cheryl said.

I gave her a big, fake smile. 'I'm not talking to you, bean-brain,' I said.

'What?' Cheryl exclaimed. 'Why, you little nerd!'

'Are you going to let that big dummy call me names?' I asked Amanda.

For a second Amanda glared at me like she wanted to tie my neck in a knot. But only for a second.

'Don't call her names,' she said to Cheryl.

Cheryl just stared at her.

'Can we get this line moving here?' shouted someone further back. 'I don't want to *die*.'

'What do you want, Stacy?' Amanda asked, her cheeks turning pink as Cheryl and Natalie stared at her in disbelief.

I nodded over to where Cindy and the

others were watching from our table. 'Bring our food over to us, please?' I asked. I gave her the list of what we all wanted to eat.

'Are you out of your tiny mind?' Natalie said, gaping at me.

'Any problems with that, Amanda?' I asked, ignoring Natalie.

'No,' Amanda said quietly. 'No problems.'

'Good.' I walked away from the line and sat down at the table with the others.

'Phew,' Cindy breathed. 'What did she say?'

I grinned.

'She said there was nothing in the world that she'd rather do than act as our waitress,' I told them. 'She said it would make her life complete.'

'She won't do it,' Fern said. 'I'll bet you.'

A couple of minutes later Amanda was heading our way with a whole tray full of stuff for us. She slammed it down on the table, her face bright red.

'Thanks,' I said. 'You can go now.' Amanda was keeping her lips tight together. I guess she was afraid that if she relaxed them she'd say what she was thinking.

And the best part of it was that her friends didn't have the faintest idea why she was waiting on me like that.

'You realize, don't you,' Pippa said after

Amanda had stalked off, 'that she's going to kill you for this, once she gets her hands on that report?'

'I'll worry about that when the time comes,' I said, handing out everyone's food. 'In the meantime, let's eat!'

Chapter Eight

We went back to my house after school to put the finishing touches to our project. We spent the afternoon writing all our notes up in our best handwriting on separate sheets and under different headings.

I did the part on migration. Those humpbacked whales sure get around. When it's winter in the north, all the humpbacks go down to the southern oceans and gorge themselves on stuff called krill. Then, in the summer, they swim thousands of miles north to find mates and produce a bunch of baby whales.

After finding out about that, I wasn't surprised they're an endangered species. They must be worn out with all that swimming. It's like spending the winter in Florida and then walking all the way to Alaska just to meet some boys.

'Have you done any more drawings?' Pippa asked.

'I haven't had time,' I said. 'I've been busy with that report for Amanda.'

'You could do one now,' Fern said. 'While we finish up.'

I wasn't too happy about starting another drawing while they were watching me. It had taken me for ever just to do that drawing of a *tail*. I wasn't sure whether I'd be able to manage an entire whale. They wanted me to copy the photograph of a forty-foot-long, thirty-ton humpback coming right out of the water.

Fern stared at my first attempt. 'It looks like a sofa standing on one end,' she said.

'Or an old beer bottle,' Pippa said. 'You know, that someone's tossed off a ship.'

'It's not as good as the other one,' Cindy said. She was being polite. It looked awful.

'We could always cut some pictures out, instead,' Fern said.

'No, we can't,' Pippa said. 'You can't cut library books up!'

'I'll *do* the drawings,' I snapped. I wasn't mad at them. I was mad at *me*. I was beginning to wish I'd never done that first drawing. Now they were expecting me to come up with some more good stuff, and I had the bad feeling that I wouldn't be able to do it. If I wasn't careful, I was going to make a complete fool of myself over these drawings.

Nightmare scene: we're all standing by our project in the swimming pool. Nat Pederson comes over.

'Hey, nice display,' he says. 'Who did the vase of flowers and the sofa?'

Humiliation!

I really wished I'd taken Amanda up on her first offer. If I hadn't been so pig-headed about doing the drawings myself I wouldn't have gotten myself into this mess.

It wasn't Amanda's fault, I knew that. But I was going to get some heavy-duty slaving out of her, anyway. At least that would make me feel a little better.

* * *

After the others had gone, I spent a while trying to draw that whale. But the harder I tried, the worse it looked. Amanda could have done something *that* good when she was five!

I gave up in the end and went downstairs to watch some TV with Mom.

'What's that noise?' Mom asked.

'I don't hear any noise,' I said.

'Sure you do.' Mom picked up the remote control and pressed the mute button. In the quiet we could hear the sound of the vacuum cleaner coming from upstairs.

'I guess Amanda's doing some vacuuming,' I said innocently.

'It sounds like it's coming from your room,' Mom said.

'Does it?' I said.

'You know darned well it does,' Mom said, frowning at me. 'What's going on in this house?'

'I guess it must be another part of "Be Nice to Younger Sisters Week",' I said.

Mom gave me a stern look. 'Come clean,' she said. 'What hold do you have over your sister?'

'I don't know what you mean,' I said. 'Amanda's just helping out. Don't you want her to help out? I thought you'd be pleased.'

'I'll start being pleased when I find out what's behind all this,' Mom said.

'There are some things it's better for a mom not to know,' I said.

Mom looked up at the ceiling then at me. She shook her head. 'OK,' she said. 'But as Amanda's being so useful around the place, I think you should do your share. Like, how long ago was it that you promised to clean the basement for me?'

'No sweat,' I said. 'Consider it done.'

'I'm out of here,' Mom said, getting up and heading for the kitchen. 'I need to make sure I'm in the right house. If you two keep carrying on like this you're going to drive me nuts.'

'We're being nice,' I told her.

'That's what I can't figure out,' Mom called from the kitchen. 'Since when have the two of you been *nice* to each other?'

Sheesh! There's no pleasing some people!

I went upstairs to my room.

Amanda was lying on my bed reading a magazine and pushing the vacuum cleaner's head up and down over the same piece of carpet, over and over.

'Hey, Sleeping Ugly!' I said. 'That part's done. How about the rest?'

Amanda sat up. She switched off the vacuum cleaner with her foot and sat on the edge of my bed looking at me.

'Can we re-negotiate this deal?' she said.

'Yes, if you like,' I said. 'We could make it a hundred hours.'

'Come on, Stacy,' Amanda pleaded. 'I bet you've already finished that report, haven't you? How about calling it even, now? I've done plenty of stuff for you. Heck, I even lent you my CD player. I mean, like, take over my *room*, why don't you? Take over my whole life!'

'You agreed to this,' I said. 'It's your own

fault. You can't back out. You know what happens to people who break their word? Their moms find out they haven't done their reports and they get kicked off the cheerleading squad.'

'OK,' Amanda said, switching the vacuum cleaner back on and shoving it around over the carpet. 'But I'm warning you, Stacy. You make me look like a fool in front of my friends again, and you won't live to see your eleventh birthday.'

'Is that a threat?' I asked.

'Yup,' Amanda said. 'It sure is.'

She looked like she meant it, too.

'OK,' I said. 'I won't embarrass you in front of your friends. You see? I can be reasonable.'

Amanda finished the vacuuming.

'Can I go now?' she said. 'Or does Her Royal Highness want me for anything else this evening?'

'There's one more thing,' I said.

Amanda growled at me. 'What?'

'Mom asked me to clean up the basement,' I told her. 'You know, all that junk at the back of her desk? It won't take you more than half an hour, tops.' I grinned at her. 'And then you can have the rest of the evening off.'

'I don't have time right now,' Amanda said. 'I'm already late for meeting the others.'

'OK,' I said generously. 'You can do it tomorrow.'

Amanda coiled up the vacuum cleaner's cord.

'I'll tell you one thing, Stacy,' she said. 'You better hope you never need any big favours from me. I'm not going to forget this.'

She walked out, dragging the vacuum cleaner behind her.

Benjamin came sliding out from under the bed. He must have hidden under there to escape the noise of the cleaner.

'You know something, Benjamin?' I said, picking him up. 'You just can't get good slaves these days.'

Chapter Nine

Amanda steered clear of me at school the next day. One second I'd see her talking to her friends or looking at a bulletin board, then *Shazam!* she'd be gone.

She wasn't even around when we went to the cafeteria. I guess she thought that if she kept out of my way she'd be safe. Wrong!

'OK, guys,' I said. 'I want everyone to come up with some chores and favours that I can get Amanda to do for me. I'm beginning to run out of ideas.'

'How about she has to do all your homework for the next week?' Fern suggested.

'Are you nuts?' I said. 'Do I look like I want to flunk out of school?'

'You could get her to comb Benjamin for fleas,' Pippa said.

'I've done that,' I said. 'Benjamin hid under my bed for three hours afterwards to recover.'

'You could toss your used clothes all over and make her pick them up and take them to the laundry room,' Cindy said. 'My folks are always bugging me about stuff like that.'

'I've done that, too,' I said.

'What about general chores around the house?' Cindy said.

'I've got that covered,' I said. 'She vacuumed my room yesterday.'

'Cleaning your shoes?' Fern said.

'How about changing Sam's diapers?' said Cindy.

'Yuck!' I said. 'Even I don't have to do that. But I could make sure she has to watch Sam next time Mom's busy. I *always* end up having to do that. Amanda's always got some excuse for getting out of it.' I grinned. 'It's kind of a mean thing to do to Sam,' I said. 'Can you imagine the sort of things she'd talk to him about?'

'Boyfriends,' Fern said.

'Hairstyles,' Pippa added.

'*Cheerleading*,' Cindy laughed. 'Poor kid!'

Poor kid or not. I was going to fix it so that Amanda had to do some baby-sitting for me before I handed over that report.

★ ★ ★

There was a lot of thumping coming from Amanda's room when I got home that afternoon. I knew what *that* meant. She was in there, practising her cheerleading in front of the mirror.

I opened her bedroom door. Sure enough, she was bouncing around, throwing her arms into the air and going: "N! A! T! P! E! D! Oh, heck! That's not right!'

'Haven't you worked it out *yet*?' I said.

She glared round at me. 'What's it to you?' she said. 'And for your information, I *have* worked it all out. I'm just perfecting it.'

'So show me,' I said. I went in and sat on her bed, curling one leg up under myself.

'Oh, sure,' Amanda said. 'So you can have a good laugh. You just don't realize how *serious* this is. We've got to do this cheer in front of a bunch of people. We'll be representing the school.'

'I won't laugh,' I said. 'Promise.'

'OK,' Amanda said. (I knew she wouldn't be able to resist showing off.) 'I've worked out these moves so that the rest of the squad forms two lines.' She drew an imaginary line of girls with her hands. They're supposed to be a diving board, right? And then I come running down the middle of the lines, like I'm preparing for a dive.' She crouched down and did this big spring into the air. 'See?' she said. 'I pretend like I'm diving off the end.'

'Uh-huh?' I said.

'And then everyone else yells "Splash!" when I land. Then we all get in line and start on the letters of Nat Pederson's name.' She went through the name. She got her legs tangled up in some tricky side-stepping on the 'R' of Pederson, and came to a wobbly stop.

'Don't you dare laugh!' she yelled.

'I'm not. I'm not.'

She started from 'P' again, and this time she managed to get through the entire name, ending up shouting 'Cham-pi-ON!' and waving her arms in the air. 'And that's how it ends,' she said breathlessly. 'See?'

'And that's it?' I said.

'Yes, that's *it*,' Amanda said. She frowned at me. 'It's the best cheer we've ever done. It'll be *amazing*! You'll see. Come on, Stacy, you could at least say something nice about it. I've worked on it like crazy.'

'I don't remember you saying anything nice about that drawing I did,' I said. 'And I worked on *that* like crazy.'

'What's that got to do with anything?' Amanda demanded. 'I wish you'd stick to the point.'

'OK,' I said. 'The cheer looks fine. If you ever manage to get through it. Have you cleaned up the basement yet, like you promised?'

'The basement?' Amanda hollered. 'Get *out* of here!' She picked up a pillow to throw at me. I ducked out of her room.

'If you don't clean the basement you don't get the report,' I reminded her. 'And if you don't get the report you won't *need* to get that cheer right. You won't even be on the squad!'

'You rat!' Amanda yelled.

'Mom wants the basement done by the weekend,' I said. I didn't hang around for her reply.

I went down to the kitchen. Mom was feeding Sam.

'Stacy, honey,' she said. 'Are you busy for a couple of hours?'

'Not really,' I said. 'Why?'

'I really ought to finish up some work I'm doing,' Mom said. 'Could you keep an eye on Sam for me while I'm downstairs?'

'Sure,' I said.

So Mom went down to her office and I took Sam into the living room for a game of Boo!

Boo! is a real simple game, but it keeps Sam amused for ages. All you have to do is lie Sam on the couch and then hide behind it. Then you come up the back of the couch and go 'Boo!' Sam laughs his head off at that one. It's almost as good as Tickle. That's where you sit on the couch and wiggle your hands over him so he doesn't know which one is going to tickle him. He thinks that's a riot. A four-alarm wriggle-and-squeal riot.

I was in the middle of this when Amanda came down the stairs.

'Where's Mom?' she asked.

'Working downstairs,' I said.

'Tell her I've gone over to Cheryl's, will you?' Amanda said.

'Hold it,' I said. 'I'm going out to see Cindy. It's your turn to stay in and watch Sam.' I'll be honest with you, I didn't have any plans to see Cindy at all. But I thought this was the perfect time to get Amanda to do some baby-sitting for me.

'Give me a break, Stacy,' Amanda said. 'It's really important that I talk to Cheryl tonight.'

'So talk to her on the phone,' I said. 'You agreed you'd do everything I asked, right? So now I'm asking you to watch Sam for me. Or don't you want that report after all?'

I could almost *see* her brain considering the choices. She could tell me to get lost and be in real big trouble at school, or she could stick to her bargain.

'How long are you going to be?' she asked.

'Who knows?' I said. 'Sam's finished eating, but he might need changing soon.'

'I'm not *changing* him,' Amanda said.

I took my jacket off the peg. 'Tell Mom I'll be back around seven,' I told her. I grinned. 'Bye, bye.'

I punched the air as I skipped into the street, just like you do when you've scored a touchdown. That was the first time I'd ever worked things so Amanda had to baby-sit Sam while I went out.

'Stay-See! Stay-See!' I chanted. 'Cham-pi-ON!'

'Stacy? Are you all right?'

I jumped halfway out of my shoes. Mr Brown from across the street was standing behind me. He must have thought I'd cracked up, the way I was waving my arms around.

'These mosquitoes are everywhere,' I said, quickly changing my waves into swattings. 'It's a wonder the whole town doesn't have malaria!'

As I walked off I could see out of the corner of my eye that Mr Brown was standing on the sidewalk with this real puzzled look on his face as he stared around for my non-existent mosquitoes.

I had the whole evening planned. I'd stroll over to Cindy's house and we'd have a good laugh at the thought of Amanda staring out through the front windows of our house like a prisoner, while Sam bounced toys off the back of her head.

There might even be some of those coconut and almond cookies that Cindy's mom bakes. And Cindy has a TV in her bedroom, so we could lie on her bed and play our channel-surfing game.

The channel-surfing game can be a real scream. It's a little like that game called 'consequences'. You know, with a folded-up piece of paper, where you write things on your turn then pass the paper to the other person without letting them see what you've written? Then they write something that *you* don't see. In the end you unfold the piece of paper and read the whole thing through. You end up with things like:

Amanda Allen MET
King Kong AT *Mount Rushmore*
SHE SAID TO HIM: *I've got ants in my pants*
HE SAID TO HER: *I love it when that happens*
AND THE CONSEQUENCE WAS: *They won the inter-state disco-dance competition.*

TV channel-surfing can be as funny as consequences, because you imagine the people talking on the different channels are having a hilarious conversation.

So, cookies, TV, and a good laugh. That was the evening I'd planned.

I rang Cindy's doorbell three or four times before I gave up. And *then* I remembered Cindy telling me her family would be out all night visiting relatives.

So much for *that* brilliant idea!

I didn't really feel like walking all the way to Pippa's house, and Fern lived even further away. Too far to walk, that's for sure.

So what was I going to do? If I went straight home, Amanda would just hand Sam back to me and be out of there before I knew it. I didn't want that happening. The whole point of this was to make the most of having Amanda as my slave.

I walked back home and peeked through the living-room window. I could see Amanda's head over the back of the couch. She was watching TV.

The question was, could I sneak in without her seeing me and sneak up to my room without her realizing I'd gotten back?

I opened the front door as quiet as a mouse.

'Sam!' I heard her saying. 'Don't pull my hair – that's a good boy.'

Shh! Close the door re-eal quiet. Tiptoe to

the stairs. Creak! I froze. Luckily the noise from the TV drowned the creaking floorboard. I hurried up the stairs and crept down the hall to my room.

Ha! I'd done it!

I closed my bedroom door.

Now, I could spend a nice quiet hour or so up there without Amanda having the faintest idea that I was in the house!

I heard the scratching noise at my door. It had to be Benjamin, wanting to get in.

I crept to the door. 'Shh!' I said, opening it a crack so he could slide through.

'Birrrow!' he said.

'Get in here and keep quiet,' I told him. 'I don't want Amanda to know I'm here.'

I'd just got myself settled on the bed with a book, when I heard someone come stampeding up the stairs. My door flew open.

'I thought so!' Amanda yelled. I sat up with a jerk and Benjamin vanished under the bed. 'I thought I heard something up here!' Amanda looked real angry.

'Don't you knock?' I said.

'You rat fink toad skunk!' Amanda yelled. 'You said you were going out!'

'I did,' I said. 'I just got back. Didn't you hear me?'

'You set this up on purpose,' Amanda hollered. 'You planned this so I'd have to stay in. I'll kill you!'

'The *report*!' I yelled. 'We've still got a deal, remember? If you kill me you'll *never* get that report, and Mom will take you off the cheerleading squad! Think of the cheerleading, Amanda!'

Amanda made some noises that sounded like a steam engine with its safety valve stuck. But she didn't say anything else. She just turned and stalked out.

As long as I kept my hands on that report I was safe. But I was beginning to wonder what Amanda might have lined up for me once I'd given it to her.

Chapter Ten

'Sta-cee? You awake?' At first I thought it was a voice in a dream. Then a hand grabbed my shoulder and shook me. Now, *voices* in dreams, I can handle, but *hands*?

I turned over right into a flashlight beam.

I blinked the sleep out of my eyes and saw a face, all eerie and creepy behind the light, with deep shadows for eyes and a fiendish grin.

Aarrgh! My worst nightmare! Zombie Sister!

I opened my mouth to yell for help.

Amanda's hand came down over my mouth. My eyes goggled.

'It's me,' Amanda hissed. 'Keep quiet! You'll wake Mom up, you ninny.' She took her hand away from my mouth and I sat up.

She was in her robe. She bent down to pick something up off the floor.

I looked at the clock by my bed. It was

almost midnight. Amanda sat on my bed and rested a box on my knees.

I reached out and switched on my light. I read the label on the box. *Mississippi Mud Pie*?

'Midnight feast,' Amanda said. 'When's the last time we had a midnight feast, huh?'

'I'm dreaming,' I said. 'This isn't really happening.'

'Are you nuts?' Amanda tore open the box and pulled out the mud pie. 'I've got a knife,' she said, reaching in her robe pocket.

'What *is* this?' I asked.

'Remember how we used to have midnight feasts in the old days?' Amanda said.

'Sure I do,' I said. 'But you were *normal* in those days.' We hadn't had a midnight feast for at least two years. The last time I'd suggested it, Amanda had told me she was too grown-up for stuff like that. What was she up to?

Amanda attacked the mud pie with the knife. The blade slid over the frozen surface. I tapped the pie with my knuckles.

'It's frozen solid,' I said. 'You'd need power tools to get through it.'

'Darn!' Amanda said. 'I didn't think it'd be *that* hard.'

I picked up the box and showed her the

label. *Defrost for two hours at room temperature before serving*.

Amanda hacked at the pie with her knife. A splinter of frozen chocolate ricochetted off the wall.

She gave me a feeble grin. 'Pretty dumb, huh?' she said.

'Pretty dumb,' I agreed.

'This stuff's too sweet, anyhow,' Amanda said.

'Huh?'

'Yeah.' She tossed her hair in an I-don't-care kind of way. 'You know how it is. When you get older you kind of lose your taste for really sweet stuff. I only brought it up here because I know you like it.'

'If this is a scam to get out of being my slave, you're wasting your time,' I told her. 'The deal still holds.'

Amanda gave me a shocked look. 'I can't believe how suspicious you are, Stacy,' she said. 'I come in here in good faith, and all you can do is accuse me of trying to trick you.'

'Yeah,' I said. 'I wonder *why*?'

'OK, forget the mud pie.' She put the rock-hard pie back in its box. 'We could talk.'

'What about?'

'I don't know,' Amanda said. '*Things*.' She

101

chewed at her bottom lip. 'How's that project of yours coming on? The whale thing?'

'It's just about finished,' I said.

'I bet it's the best whale project ever, huh?' she said. 'I bet you get an "A" for it.' She sighed like someone in a really cheap soap opera. 'I wish I was as smart at school stuff as you are, Stacy. It must be great to have a brain.'

I wrapped my arm around myself and went, 'Brrr!'

'You cold?' Amanda asked.

'It's this snow job you're giving me.'

'I'm being honest, here, Stacy,' Amanda said. 'Like . . . I mean, I really wish I was smart enough to have done that book report the way you did it. Like, wow, that was really something. You read that book and had that report written in, like, *no* time flat. And I bet it's a really good report, too, huh, Stacy?'

'Don't sweat it, Amanda,' I said. 'I made some deliberate spelling mistakes so they'd think it was you.'

'There's nothing wrong with my spelling!' Amanda said.

'Oh, sure. Spell February, Amanda.'

She breathed out hard through her nose. Snort! 'I was thinking,' she said. 'I suppose you've got the report somewhere *safe*, haven't

102

you?' She looked around my room. 'I mean, you haven't just left it lying around somewhere? I wouldn't want you to lose it or anything.'

'It's safe,' I said, glancing over at my desk.

'Uh-huh?' Amanda nodded. 'Great.'

'Can I go back to sleep now?' I asked. 'Or are we going to chat some more?'

She stood up and picked up the mud pie box. 'I'll stash this under your bed,' she said. 'You can have it for breakfast tomorrow, if you feel like it.'

Mississippi Mud Pie for breakfast?

She slid the box under my bed and headed for the door.

'Hey, Amanda?' I said. 'Next time you want to bribe me, trying fixing it so I can actually *eat* the bribe.'

'Nice joke,' she said. She gave me a smile and crept out.

Now, there's subtle, there's not-so-subtle, there's really *obvious*, and there's Amanda. Frozen Mississippi Mud Pie! I mean, come *on*!

I got out of bed and took the finished book report out of my desk drawer. I carefully folded it in half and slipped it under my pillow. I wasn't taking any chances.

Saturday morning, I yanked the mud pie out but it looked kind of soggy after a night under my bed, so I just kicked it back under there, meaning to put it back in the freezer later in the hope that it'd firm up a little.

I met Amanda out in the hall.

'Do you want to use the bathroom first, Stacy?' Amanda asked me. We don't have our usual early morning fight for the bathroom on a Saturday, so her offer wasn't any big deal. Still, why not?

'Thanks,' I said, not letting her see that I knew she was up to something. I went in there, counted to twenty, then crept out along the hall. I *knew* it! Amanda was in my room over at my desk, carefully opening the drawers. Any second now she'd find it. She pulled out the centre drawer.

'Funn-ee!' she said.

I zipped back to the bathroom before she saw me.

I'd left her a little note in thick red magic marker on a sheet of paper I'd put in my middle drawer. It said: *SORRY, YOUR REPORT IS NOT IN HERE.*

She came down to breakfast looking real glum.

'Are you OK, honey?' Mom asked her.

'Oh, just fine,' Amanda said, sitting at the table.

'Maybe she didn't sleep too well,' I said. 'Did you sleep OK, Amanda?'

'I slept fine,' Amanda said. 'As well as anyone could sleep with the threat of being taken off the cheerleading squad hanging over them.'

'All you've got to do is finish that report,' Mom said. 'Are you having problems with it?'

'No,' Amanda said quickly. 'I'm not having any problems. What problems? It's a *breeze*!'

'Have you finished it yet?' I asked innocently.

'Not quite,' she said icily. 'I've just got one or two things left to do. One or two loose ends to sort out and then I'll be *completely* finished.'

She gave me a frosty smile. As frosty as that Mississippi Mud Pie had been. Amanda was not in a good mood that morning.

★ ★ ★

You know, I think some people have a definite talent for being in command. The leader of the pack. The big cheese. All those years I'd spent trying to get out from under Amanda, and do you know what she was doing right then?

Well, I was on the rug in the living room watching TV and eating some peanuts. And Amanda? She was down in the basement cleaning the place up for me.

Mom was out with Sam, visiting some neighbours. I took a handful of peanuts and chewed happily. It was great having a slave.

The phone rang. I dragged it over to the TV.

'Hello?'

'Is Amanda there?' I'd recognize that squeaky voice anywhere. It was Rachel Goldstein.

'I'm afraid Amanda is busy right now,' I said. 'Can I take a message?'

'Oh, sure. Can you tell her we're meeting up at the Happy Donut at six o'clock?' Rachel said. 'And tell her Greg will be there.'

The Happy Donut is the hangout where the Bimbos meet up on Saturday evenings to swap Bimbo-talk.

'Leave it to me,' I said.

'Make sure you tell her *Greg* will be there,' Rachel said. 'Six o'clock sharp, OK?'

I put the phone down. I had the feeling I'd heard something about a boy named Greg before. I didn't give it any more thought. If I had, I might have remembered that Greg was the boy Amanda has sounded so excited about the other morning. The one with the sister named Karen. Remember?

I went back to my peanuts and the TV.

Now, I don't want you thinking I forgot to give Amanda the message on purpose. I just *forgot*. I mean, a person has got other things to think about, right? A person could spend her whole life giving Amanda messages.

Mom got home later in the afternoon. After we'd all eaten, Mom put Sam to bed and got out the Scrabble board on the rug in the living room.

Amanda was up in her room. We didn't bother calling her down. She doesn't like Scrabble much, especially not when Mom is playing. Amanda and I play together sometimes, but I always win. Word games aren't really Amanda's idea of fun. She hasn't got what you'd call an enormous vocabulary, and she's not very good at spelling either. She always misses the first 'R' in February, and that's just for starters.

It was much later when Amanda came wandering down.

'Mom? Has anyone called me?' she asked.

'Not since I've been home, honey,' Mom said. 'Stacy, what kind of word is that?'

'FLUP,' I spelled. 'It's a real word, honest.'

'Get out of here!' Mom said. 'You cheat worse than your father.'

'I don't get it,' Amanda said. 'Rachel said she'd call.'

'Oh, yeah,' I said. 'She did. Sorry. I forgot to tell you.'

'What? When?' Amanda sounded really anxious. 'What did she say?'

'Something about the Happy Donut,' I told her. 'I'm sorry. I forgot all about it.'

'But what did she *say?*' Amanda howled.

'Something about them meeting up at six o'clock,' I said. I spread out my letters again. PLUFF. 'Now, that's *definitely* a real word,' I told Mom.

'Hmm,' Mom said.

'Stacy, will you quit it with that dumb game!' Amanda yelled. 'Who did Rachel say was meeting there?'

'No one in particular,' I said. 'Oh, wait a minute, though. She did say some guy's name.'

Amanda's face went white. 'Not . . . not Greg?'

'Yes, that was it. Greg.'

Amanda let out a howl that sounded like a wolf baying at the full moon. 'Oh, no!' she screamed. 'Six o'clock? That was two hours ago! You did this on purpose!'

'Amanda, honey,' Mom said. 'Calm down. I'm sure Stacy didn't forget on purpose.'

'Of course she did!' Amanda yelled. 'That's it! She's ruined my life! I might as well go *kill* myself now!' She looked at the wall clock. 'I might still be able to get down there.'

'You're not going out at this time of night, Amanda,' Mom said.

'You don't understand!' Amanda hollered. 'I'll never see him again. Never! I hate you, Stacy Allen! I absolutely *hate* you!' She ran upstairs and the whole house shook as she slammed her bedroom door.

'Phew!' I said. 'Some people!'

Mom gave me a stern look. 'Did you forget to give her that message on purpose, Stacy?' she asked in her best no-nonsense voice.

'Of course not,' I said.

'Hmm!' Mom said.

A picture is supposed to say a thousand words. I don't know about that, but I can tell you one thing for sure. One of my Mom's 'hmm's can say a *million* words.

'I'd better go check on her,' Mom said. She got up off the rug. 'And no cheating while I'm gone, Stacy.'

'Would I?' I said. 'And, hey, I really did forget that message, Mom.'

'I hope so,' Mom said. 'I wouldn't want to

think you were the sort of person to play a spiteful trick like that.'

That made me feel terrible.

But I had really, honestly, *genuinely* forgotten.

Surely Amanda couldn't be *that* upset about it?

Could she?

Chapter Eleven

Things were ominously quiet upstairs. I looked at the letters on my Scrabble letter holder. XQWRKZY.

The way I saw it, I had three options:

1. *Try making something out of the letters I've got.* In other words, let Mom hammer me into the carpet.
2. *Swap some of my more useless letters for ones still in the unused letter bag.* This particular strategy is known as cheating.
3. *Convince Mom that Xqwrkzy is a real word.* We call *this* little trick Creative Scrabbling.

Xqwrkzy: A rare species of Venezuelan bull-frog. This little critter makes its nest in the branches of the tropical rainforest and is noted for its high-pitched mating call, which bears remarkable similarity to the melody of

'Follow the Yellow Brick Road' from The Wizard of Oz.

Now, Amanda might go for that, but *Mom*? Mom was gone for about ten minutes. I couldn't hear any yelling from Amanda, which was unusual. When Amanda's real mad about something, she normally lets the entire neighbourhood know.

Mom came back down.

'Tempest in a teapot, huh?' I said. I'd heard Mom use that expression about Amanda's tantrums in the past.

'She's upset, Stacy,' Mom said, frowning at me.

'Mad, you mean?' I said.

'No.' Mom sat down on the rug. 'Just upset. She'll get over it.'

'Over what?' I couldn't understand what all the fuss was about.

'She was hoping this Greg guy was going to ask her out.' Mom said. 'But now she's convinced he'll ask Natalie or Rachel out instead.'

'You mean out, like, on a date?' I said.

'I guess that was the idea,' Mom said.

'Amanda wants to date a *boy*?' I said. 'She doesn't *date*. She's never *dated*.'

Sure, Amanda and her friends were always

talking about boys, but Amanda had never actually been on a *date* with one.

'She's growing up, honey,' Mom said. 'She was bound to start showing an interest in boys at some stage.'

Wow! My big sister was interested in *dating*? She was growing up? It had to happen some time? Sheesh! The next thing I knew she'd be engaged. She'd be getting married. She'd move out. No more Amanda. The idea didn't appeal to me at *all*.

'You wouldn't let her, Mom, would you?' I asked. I know I don't always get along with Amanda, but I sure didn't like the idea of not having her around any more.

Who would there be to argue with? Who would there be for me to beat at Scrabble? Amanda was the only person in the whole world who'd have believed that a *Xqwrkzy* was a Venezuelan bullfrog.

'I can't think of any reason why not,' Mom said with a strange little smile. 'Why are you so jumpy about it, honey?'

'I'm not,' I said frantically. 'Why should I be? Amanda can date if she wants to. It doesn't bother me.'

'Stacy,' Mom said. 'Calm down. Amanda's thirteen. It's perfectly normal for her to be interested in boys. You'll see, in a couple of years, you'll be just the same.'

'I won't!' I said. 'Never!' The thirty-month gap between Amanda and me suddenly felt like thirty *years*. Amanda was a *teenager*. A teenager who wanted to date boys.

'Why can't stuff stay the *same*?' I said miserably.

Mom gave me a hug. 'Dating boys is no big problem,' she said. 'Nothing's going to change around here. Not for years and years.'

'Yes it will,' I said. 'Amanda will meet some boy she really likes, and then she'll get married and have kids. That'll make me an *aunt*. I'm too young to be an aunt.'

'And Amanda's too young to be getting married. That won't happen for a long time,' Mom said. 'Now, come on, Stacy, how about you and me finishing our game?'

'OK,' I said. 'But I won't be able to concentrate.' I put down my pieces.

'CUSHION,' Mom read. 'Hey, a seven-letter word, Stacy. And on a triple-score square. Good for you!'

I smiled. Well, who's to know?

Oh, by the way, Mom still won!

*　*　*

I knocked on Amanda's bedroom door.

'Amanda? It's me,' I called. 'Can I come in?'

I heard some noises from inside her room and then this real miserable-sounding voice said, 'Come in if you *must*.'

She was lying on her bed, facing the wall.

'Amanda? I'm sorry about forgetting that message,' I said.

She sighed dramatically. 'It doesn't matter,' she said.

I felt terrible. Mom had been right. She wasn't mad at me at all.

'You can yell at me if it'll make you feel better,' I told her. 'I won't yell back. I promise. I won't say a word.'

I had to make friends with her. I didn't want her to go off and get married and stuff. (OK, so I was overreacting a little, but girls with unhappy home lives *do* run away with boys. I'd read about it in one of Amanda's magazines. I didn't want to be the one who made her home life so miserable that she ended up eloping with this Greg guy.)

'I don't want to yell at you,' Amanda sighed.

'Sure you do,' I said. 'You can even call me metal-mouth. How about that, Amanda? Don't you want to call me metal-mouth?'

'No,' she said quietly.

This was bad. This was mega-serious.

I stood there looking at her back for a while. That was when I had the idea. I knew what to do.

'Don't go away,' I said. 'I've got something for you.'

I ran back to my room and pulled the book report out from under my pillow.

I went back to her room.

'Hey, Amanda?' I said. 'Look. It's the report. You can have it.' She didn't even look around. I put it on the bed behind her. 'And you don't have to be my slave any more,' I told her. 'We can just forget about it, huh?'

Her shoulders went up and down with another big sigh.

'Amanda?'

'Look, can you just leave me alone for a while?' she said. 'I'm not in the mood for talking right now.'

I backed away. 'Sure,' I said. 'But if there's anything I can do, just holler, OK?'

No reply. I closed her door real quietly and went back to my room. Benjamin was curled up on my bed. I sat next to him and gave him a big stroke.

'I'm going to be real nice to Amanda from now on,' I told him. 'Cross my heart and hope to die.'

Sunday is one of my favourite days. Especially when there's no chores, and no homework to do. And this Sunday was especially exciting, because I knew that somewhere on the highway between Chicago and Four Corners, Dad was in his car on his way home.

I met up with my friends in the morning and we did some window-shopping at the mall. We ended up spending most of the morning there. I kept looking at my watch, counting down the time until Dad would be home.

His car still wasn't in the driveway when I got home.

'You said he'd be here at noon,' I said to Mom.

'I said this afternoon,' Mom said. 'He'll be here soon. Don't worry.'

I had lunch, then spent a while up in my room, reading and playing with Benjamin. It was real quiet downstairs, which is how come I heard Amanda talking on the telephone.

She's got this habit of lying all over the stairs when she's having one of her long Bimbo-blabs with her friends and I was on my way to the bathroom, so I wasn't exactly eaves-dropping.

'He said *what*?' Amanda squealed. I could

see her down there, twisting the phone cord around her hand. 'I didn't think he'd even *noticed* me!' She was squirming like she had an itch. She *had* to be talking about Greg.

'He said that? He actually said *that*?' Amanda said after a short pause. 'Oh! I wish I'd *been* there! That's just *so* annoying. Yes, I *know* I said I'd be there. It was Stacy's fault. I didn't get the message until it was too late.'

There was another pause. 'Yeah! Kid sisters, huh? Tell me about it! It's not as if she couldn't have called me, I was only down in the base-ment doing *her* cleaning.' Pause. 'Oh, I'll tell you about it some other time. We had this deal, but I guess I can forget all about *that* now. Stacy's feeling real guilty, so I'm not going to have any trouble with *her* for a while. But tell me some more about Greg. Did he really say I had the cutest smile he'd ever seen?'

I'd heard enough by then. Judging by what Amanda was saying, it sounded like she'd been the main topic of conversation over at the Happy Donut yesterday, even *without* being there. The cutest smile he'd ever seen? Greg thought *that*? No wonder Amanda was wrig-gling about down there.

What annoyed me though was Amanda's comment about me feeling guilty. About her not having any *trouble* with me any more. OK, so I *had* felt guilty. Of course I had. That's why I'd given her the report. And maybe her slaving days *were* over, but if she thought I'd be feeling guilty for long, she was wrong.

And she'd called me her 'kid sister'. If there's one thing that really annoys me, it's being referred to as her kid sister!

I waited until she'd finished on the phone, then I went down to the kitchen. So she thought I was a kid, did she? I had an idea for getting even about *that* little comment. I'd show her how much of a *kid* I could be.

One of Amanda's irritating habits is that she's always coming up when I'm eating or drinking something and sneaking stuff off my plate or taking a slurp out of my glass. Remember that cherry pie?

It drives me crazy, but right now it was going to be a habit I could make good use of with a bit of imaginative milkshake mixing.

I fixed myself a banana shake. Banana à la Boom! I went through all of the kitchen cupboards, spooning in plenty of interesting new flavours.

Banana à la Boom
Ingredients:
- *Half a pint of milk.*

- *Two heaped spoonfuls of banana milkshake powder.*
- *A pinch – or twelve – of pepper.*
- *A spoonful of mustard.*
- *Four spoonfuls of salt.*
- *Ten shakes of Tabasco.*
- *A spoonful of curry powder.*
- *A spoonful of chili powder.*

Mix thoroughly, stand back and wait for your sister to come in and take a slurp. Kapow!

Kid sister strikes back! And how!

Chapter Twelve

The trap was set. The innocent-looking glass of milkshake was sitting on the table. All it needed now was for the *victim* to walk unsuspectingly into my fiendish trap. Nya-ha-harr! (That was fiendish laughter, in case you couldn't tell.)

'Mrrp.'

I looked round. 'Hi, Benjamin,' I said as he came padding into the kitchen. I knelt down to play with him.

'Have I got a surprise for that sister of ours!' I told him. 'You just hang around in here. She's going to be the first thirteen-year-old in orbit when she tastes that shake.'

'Mrr mowr mrrp mrower,' Benjamin said, rubbing up against me.

'You can say that again,' I told him. 'Wait up – I'll get you some food.'

I was just hacking up his cat chunks with a fork when I heard Amanda coming down the stairs.

She came into the kitchen.

'Hi, Stacy.'

I didn't say anything.

'Hi, Stacy!'

'Do you need some fresh water, honey-bunny?' I asked Benjamin. I picked up his bowl and went over to the sink.

'*Stacy!* HI!' Amanda came over and waved her hand in front of my face. 'Hello? Anyone home?'

'Excuse me,' I said very stiffly. 'You're in my way.'

'It speaks!' Amanda said. 'It's a miracle!'

'Are you going to get out of my way, or what?' I asked.

'What's the problem, Stacy?' Amanda asked.

'I don't like being called a kid,' I said.

She frowned at me. 'You *are* a kid,' she said. 'Anyway, who's been calling you a kid?'

'*You!*' I said. 'I heard you. On the phone.'

'Oh, Stacy! That was nothing,' she said with a shrug. 'Anyway, you shouldn't have been listening. You know what Mom says: "Eavesdroppers never hear things properly".'

' "Eavesdroppers never hear any good about themselves",' I corrected her. 'That's what Mom says. Anyway, I wasn't eavesdropping.

122

They could probably hear you in Canada, the way you were shouting.'

'If it's such a big deal, then I'm sorry,' Amanda said. 'OK? Did you hear me? I *apologize* for calling you a kid.'

'You're in a pretty good mood all of a sudden,' I said. 'What happened? Did Greg ask you out after all?'

Amanda grinned from ear to ear. 'Not exactly,' she said. 'But he didn't ask Cheryl or any of the others out, and Natalie said he was talking about me all night. He said he thinks I've got—'

'The cutest smile in the whole wide world,' I finished for her. 'Yeah. I heard. Tell me, is this Greg guy really stupid or is he blind?'

Amanda leaned against the worktop. 'Nope,' she said. 'He's got these really nice blue eyes.' She sighed. 'And he's tall and really good-looking. I could really *go* for him.'

'Go?' I said, trying to sound unimpressed. 'Go where?'

Amanda giggled. 'Oh, *anywhere*,' she sighed. She wandered dreamily around the kitchen.

'Excuse me while I go and throw up,' I said. 'This is getting really nauseating.'

She smiled. 'You wouldn't understand,' she said. 'You're only a kid.'

'There you go again,' I said. 'Calling me a kid.'

'Sorry,' Amanda said.

'Have you copied that report yet?' I asked. I wanted to remind her of the sacrifice I'd made for her.

'No. Not yet,' Amanda said, sitting down at the table. 'There's plenty of time.' She reached out and nudged the glass of explosive shake around with her fingers. I held my breath.

'I hope you don't forget how I let you off your side of our deal,' I said, trying not to stare at the shake as she edged it around the table absent-mindedly. *Drink it*, I was thinking. *Go ahead and drink it!*

'I did enough work for you,' Amanda said. 'They could have used a slave-driver like you in ancient Egypt. You know, building the pyramids. Is there any orange juice in the fridge?'

'I didn't see any,' I lied. 'You can have some of my shake if you like.'

'Thanks.' This was it! Woo-hah! Stand by for blast-off!

Amanda picked up the glass.

Five . . . four . . . three . . . two . . .

Amanda looked into the glass and her nose wrinkled up.

'What the heck are all these red things, Stacy?' she said. 'It looks like it has measles.'

She sniffed at the shake. 'Ew! What did you *put* in here?'

'Banana,' I said.

'Sheesh! You should get that banana analysed, Stacy, it's got to be some kind of mutant.' She sniffed again, then this big grin spread over her face. 'Nice try, Stacy,' she said. 'Real cute. What is it? Chili powder?'

'It adds to the flavour,' I said. The jig was up, what the heck? I grinned at her. 'Haven't you ever heard of chili-banana flavour? It's a new line down at the supermarket.'

'Did you really think I'd be dumb enough to actually *drink* this gunk?' Amanda said.

'Do you want an honest answer?' I asked.

Amanda came round the table, holding the glass towards me. 'You drink it,' she said.

Just then we heard the honking of a car horn out front.

'Dad!' I yelled.

Amanda put the glass down and ran behind me to the front door. It was! It was Dad. He was just getting out of the car.

My dad is really tall and broad. I mean, he's *huge*. When he puts his arms around you it's like being hugged by a *bear*. He slammed the car door and held out his arms for us.

'My favourite girls!' he called, his face one big smile.

We galloped down the driveway, nearly bowling him over in our rush to get to him. I jumped at him and he caught me in mid-air, swinging me around.

'Yeayyy!' I yelled. 'You're *home*!'

'You can say that again,' Dad said in his big brown bear voice. 'For eight whole days. Where's your mom? How's your brother?'

We helped him indoors with his bags.

He gave Mom a huge hug. It was perfect! Dad was home and we were a family again.

We dumped his bags and went into the kitchen.

'I'll get Sam,' I said, dancing around Dad.

'How is he?' Dad asked. 'Does he know any words yet?'

'He knows "gaaga",' said Amanda.

'I've missed you so much,' Dad said. 'All of you. Three whole weeks without my girls!' He looked around the kitchen and gave a big, happy sigh. 'Whoo!' he said. 'Milkshake! That's just what I need right now!'

I was halfway out of the kitchen, heading to get Sam from his crib. I spun around in time to see Dad grab the glass up off the kitchen table.

'No!' Amanda and I yelled at the same time.

Dad didn't stop to look at it. He didn't stop

to sniff it. He just put it to his mouth and drank.

You know when it's snowed really heavily and they get out these big snow-blower machines? You know, the ones that suck all the snow up off the roads and blow it out the side? Well, if you've seen one of those things in action, you'll have a pretty good idea of what happened with that mouthful of milkshake.

Bleergh! Mega-spray all over the table and Dad coughing and choking and going bright red. He sort of collapsed into a chair, fighting for breath.

'Stacy! You idiot!' Amanda yelled.

'*Ugg! Gugg! Glaaahhh!*' Dad gasped, waving his arms. 'Wah . . . wah . . . water!'

I ran and got him a glass of water. Mom was just staring at us with her mouth hanging open. Dad took a long drink, tears pouring down his face.

'I was playing a trick on Amanda,' I said. 'It wasn't meant for *you*!'

It was a little while before Dad could say anything. He wiped the tears out of his eyes and took a few deep breaths.

'I . . . *ugg* . . . Stacy! *Yecch*! Some welcome home!'

Mom glared at me. 'Stacy, why on earth did you do that?'

'I was supposed to get it,' Amanda said.

'For what?' Dad gasped. 'What the heck did you do to deserve *that*?'

'Nothing,' Amanda said.

A couple more coughs and another drink of water and Dad had almost recovered.

'Nothing?' he said. 'This time-bomb was for *nothing*?'

'I called her a kid,' Amanda said. 'That's all.'

Mom gave me a ferocious look. 'Stacy,' she said, 'there are times when I really wonder about you.'

'It was only a joke,' I said.

'That's right,' Amanda said. 'It was only a joke.'

Dad wiped his eyes. He began to laugh.

'It's got quite a kick, Stacy,' he said. 'Maybe you've got a future mixing cocktails. You should call this one the Stacy Allen Throat Buster.'

'Are you OK, honey?' Mom asked him.

'I'm fine,' Dad said, with another laugh. 'It's great to be home!'

We all laughed then. That's the really great thing about my dad. He doesn't get anything like as mad as Mom would. If she'd taken a swig of that shake I'd have been *murdered*.

'Get a cloth,' Mom said to me, laughing along with the rest of us. 'You can wipe this mess up, Stacy. And no more tricks, hear me?'

'I promise,' I said. 'No more tricks.'

★ ★ ★

We spent the afternoon swapping news.

Dad sat on the couch, bouncing Sam on his knees and telling us all the things he'd been doing in Chicago.

Then we told him everything we'd been doing.

Dad had bought everyone presents. He doesn't always bring presents back, so that was a real nice surprise. He said it was because he'd made a big sale.

'Does that mean we're rich enough for you to come back and work from home?' Amanda asked, sitting on the floor at his feet.

'Not just yet,' Dad said. 'But one day I will be. I don't want to be away from you for *one second* longer than I have to be.' He'd brought Mom back a red silk scarf. Amanda had a silver brooch in the shape of a rearing horse, and I had a new china pig for my collection.

Sam had a big box of coloured building blocks. He seemed more interested in sucking them than building anything with them, but I guessed he'd grow into them.

'Is anyone starting to get hungry?' Mom asked with a smile. 'There's a Mississippi Mud Pie in the freezer. We can have it for dessert.'

Uh-oh! Oh, no there wasn't. There was a Mississippi Mud Pie *under my bed*, but there wasn't one in the freezer. Not unless Mom had bought two.

'How about if you go and get it out to defrost, Stacy?' Mom asked.

I looked at Amanda. She stared blankly at me for a moment, then her hand came up over her mouth.

'Did you put it back?' she whispered to me.

I shook my head.

'What's going on?' Mom asked.

'Um, nothing,' I said, getting up. 'It's OK. I'll get it.'

'Put it on a high shelf,' called Mom. 'We don't want the cat getting at it.'

'Do cats eat Mississippi Mud Pies?' I heard Dad ask as I detoured from the kitchen and crept upstairs.

'That cat would eat anything,' I heard Mom say.

I tiptoed into my room.

Benjamin came streaking out from under my bed, his whiskers covered in cream.

I looked under the bed. The answer to Dad's question was staring me in the face through the open box.

Yes, cats *do* eat Mississippi Mud Pie. At least, they lick the cream off the top.

I groaned as I dragged the pie out. It looked like I had a lot of explaining to do. Thanks to Benjamin. But thanks mostly to Amanda for bringing it up here in the first place.

I picked the box up and went downstairs.

Thanks, Amanda. Thanks a *bunch*.

Chapter Thirteen

One of the really good things about having Dad home is that it puts Mom in a permanent good mood.

Take the incident with the Mississippi Mush Pie.

'How did the cat get at it?' Mom asked.

'I guess he must have sniffed it out,' I said. 'You know what a nose he's got for food.'

'I didn't see it in the kitchen anywhere,' Mom said.

'It wasn't exactly in the kitchen,' Amanda said.

'It was in my room,' I said. 'Under my bed.'

Mom gave Dad a blank look. 'Under your bed?' she said. 'And what was it doing under your bed?'

'Defrosting,' Amanda said helpfully.

'I forgot it was there,' I told Mom. 'I meant to put it back in the freezer, but I forgot.'

'OK,' Mom said. She was obviously having

problems with this. 'Let's start over. Why did you put it under your bed in the first place?'

'I didn't,' I said. 'Amanda did.'

Mom looked at Amanda.

'It was frozen solid,' Amanda explained. 'You have to let it defrost for two hours. It says so on the label.'

'So we couldn't eat it right away,' I said. 'It was as hard as rock.'

'So you put it under your bed to defrost?' Mom said very slowly.

'That's right,' I said. 'And then I forgot all about it. Maybe it'll be OK if we scrape off the bits that Benjamin has eaten?'

'I'm not eating something the cat's licked,' Amanda said. 'Couldn't we have ice-cream instead?'

Mom looked from me to Amanda. 'I give up,' she said. 'I'm not even going to *try* to figure this out.'

We had cookies-and-cream ice-cream for dessert. Mom never did find out how the Mississippi Mud Pie got under my bed.

* * *

Later that evening I took Dad up to my room to show him our whale project.

He sat on the bed while I spread it out on the carpet. He was very impressed with all the

133

work we'd done. There were six different topic headings, each written out real neat on a separate sheet, and Pippa had even managed a pretty good map showing how the whales migrate.

I included the good drawing I'd done of the whale tail, and the bad one of the whole whale coming up out of the sea.

'I'm still working on that drawing,' I told him. 'It's a lot harder than the tail.'

'I guess so,' Dad said. 'Why don't you ask Amanda to help you with it?'

'Because it's *our* project,' I said. 'It wouldn't be the same if Amanda did the drawings.'

'I didn't mean you should get Amanda to *do* the drawing,' Dad said. 'But she could give you a few tips on how to go about it. You should never be too proud to ask for advice, Stacy. Especially when there's someone nearby who knows more about something than you do. I mean, you help Amanda out with her schoolwork sometimes, don't you?'

I gave him a careful look. 'Sometimes,' I said. 'If she asks.'

Dad gave me a long, slow look. I felt a little uncomfortable. It was like he was trying to tell me something without actually *saying* it.

'I was talking to your mom earlier,' he said.

134

'She was telling me how Amanda has been doing your chores for you.'

I began to feel a little squirmy.

'Uh-huh,' I said, staring down at the project so I didn't have to look into his eyes. I knew that if I looked straight at him, I'd want to confess everything. Dad has that effect on me. I don't know why. He just does.

'Normie Perkins!' Dad said suddenly.

I looked at him. 'Huh?'

'Normie Perkins,' he repeated. 'He was a kid at my school. He used to run a homework service for the other kids in class. We'd pay him to do our homework for us. Sometimes we gave him money, but more often, he'd get us to do things for him as payment.' Dad smiled. 'He had quite a little racket going. We all thought it was a great idea. We'd give him our homework, and he'd do it for us while we were out playing baseball in the park.' Dad smiled at me. 'What do you think of that, huh?'

'I'm not sure,' I said. 'It sounds kind of like cheating.'

'Why do you think that?' Dad asked. 'What harm could it do?'

'Well,' I said thoughtfully. 'If none of the other guys did the work, they wouldn't *learn* the stuff, would they?'

'You know,' Dad said. 'That's exactly what my mother told me when she found out about it. "You're never going to learn anything," she said, "unless you do the work *yourself*." You see, she was all for us kids getting together and helping one another, but for one kid to do *all* our work while the rest of us goofed off in the park, well, that was something else. That was a real bad idea, according to my mom.' Dad looked at me. 'What do you think?'

I looked straight into my Dad's eyes. 'I guess she was right,' I mumbled.

'We thought Normie was doing us a big favour,' Dad said. 'But he wasn't. He was just making it harder for us in the long run.' He stood up. 'Helping people out is fine,' he said. 'Doing their work in return for favours isn't.' He smiled and patted my hair. 'I still think you should ask Amanda to help with your drawing, sweetheart,' he said.

He left me sitting on the floor in there. I couldn't tell whether he'd figured out what was going on between me and Amanda, but he was sure hot on the trail. And what was much worse was that he'd made me feel real bad about the whole deal I'd cooked up with Amanda.

But what could I do about it? I'd already given Amanda the report.

It sure is hard sometimes, when you realize you've done something wrong, but you can't come up with any way of undoing it.

★ ★ ★

A little while later there was a rattle of fingers on my door and Amanda came in. She looked kind of thoughtful. It didn't take a genius to figure out why.

'Has Dad been talking to you?' I asked.

'He told me about some kid called Normie Perkins,' Amanda said, sitting dejectedly on my bed.

I nodded. 'Me too,' I told her.

'Mom must have told him about all the stuff I was doing for you,' Amanda said. 'And about the book report I was supposed to be doing. Dad didn't actually *say* anything about that, but that only makes it worse. Do you think they've figured it all out?'

'I guess so,' I said.

Amanda sighed. 'How come I feel so bad about it?' she said. 'It seemed like a really good idea at the time.'

'I know what you mean,' I said.

'I guess I should read that book myself, huh?' Amanda said. 'I'll have to ask Mr

Townes to give me a few more days over it. At least I finished the project on the Great Lakes – that's something.' She reached into her pocket and pulled my crumpled report out. 'You'd better have this back.'

I took it from her. 'Hey,' I said. 'Once you've read the book, we could work on your report together, couldn't we? Dad said we should help each other.'

She looked at me. 'Would you do that?' she said.

'Sure,' I said with a grin. 'On one condition.'

'No way!' she said. 'I'm not making any more deals with you. You can forget about that.'

'You'll like *this* deal,' I said. I looked at my attempt at drawing the whale coming out of the sea. 'I can't *do* it,' I said. 'I've tried and tried, but it just won't come out right.'

Amanda looked at the drawing.

'Show me the picture,' she said.

I got the library book out and opened it to the right page.

'Have you got some clean paper?' Amanda asked. 'And a pencil?'

'Yup,' I said, getting up and going over to my desk. I looked at her over my shoulder.

'But I don't want you to *do* the drawing for me. Just show me what I'm doing wrong, OK?'

Amanda smiled. 'Deal,' she said.

'And I'll help you with your report,' I said.

Amanda looked up. 'Wait a minute,' she said. 'This still doesn't add up.'

'Sure it does,' I said. 'You help me with my drawings, and I help you with your report. What's the problem?'

'The problem is that I've just spent most of this week slaving my socks off for you,' Amanda said. 'So no matter how you figure it, I'm getting ripped off.'

This was true.

'OK,' I said. 'I'll help you with your report, *and* I'll do some of your chores next week. How's that?'

Amanda grinned. 'Fine. I can't wait to come up with some chores for you!' she said. 'A nice long list.'

'Hey, don't go crazy,' I said.

But what could I do? I'd sure worked *her* into the ground. And now the tables were turned. It looked like Amanda was about to get herself a new slave.

Me and my brilliant ideas.

Chapter Fourteen

First thing on Tuesday morning, a whole bunch of us were lined up outside the school, waiting for the bus to take us to the swim meet. I had our humpbacked whale project in an art folder that Amanda had lent me. That way I could keep it all flat and save it from getting dog-eared and creased in my bag.

Amanda had really helped me a lot with my drawing. It was all pretty obvious stuff, once she had actually pointed it out to me. You know, like judging the distance from the tip of a whale's nose way back to its eye – which is a lot further back than you'd think.

It's amazing how you can look at a photograph and think you're copying it right when you *aren't*. Stuff like getting the hump in the right place. And drawing the water so it really looks like it might be wet. Amanda explained how to do all kinds of stuff like that. But I did all the actual drawing.

Don't get me wrong. I'm never going to be

an artist, but by the time I'd finished that drawing late Monday night, no one in the world was going to say it looked like a sofa standing on one end.

It looked like a humpbacked whale. No kidding, it looked just like a humpbacked whale. And boy, was I proud of myself!

Cindy and the others were amazed when I gave them a sneak preview.

'And you said you couldn't draw,' Fern said. She gave me a suspicious look. 'Are you sure you did this? It didn't look anything *like* this good the other day.'

'Amanda helped,' I said.

'I knew it!' Fern said.

'She didn't *draw* it,' I said. 'I drew every line myself. She just gave me some advice.'

'What did *that* cost?' Cindy asked.

I told them about the conversation I'd had with my dad, and about the new deal I'd worked out with Amanda.

The only part of the new deal I didn't tell anyone about was the fact that I'd agreed to do Amanda's chores for the rest of the week. I decided to keep that one to myself. There are some things you don't want even your very best friends to know about, after all.

★ ★ ★

It was total chaos in the foyer at the swimming pool that morning. We'd brought a bunch of free-standing screens to pin our projects up on, but there wasn't enough space for them all around the walls, so we had to make it into a series of walkways with screens on either side in order to fit everything in.

Ms Fenwick and a couple of other teachers helped out with the arrangements, sorting out who got what screen, and how much room we were allowed.

Betsy-Jane Garside's project included a huge painted dolphin, about two yards long. The people on either side of her complained about her taking up their space, so in the end they made Betsy-Jane's dolphin into the centrepiece. Great. The first thing anyone walking in through the doors would see was Betsy-Jane's dolphin.

Cindy, Fern, Pippa and I pinned up our stuff, then did a tour of the exhibition to see how all the others had done. Most of them were pretty good, but I thought our presentation was one of the best.

Most of them had done drawings. There are guys in my class who are really good at drawing. Andy Melniker, for instance. And Larry Franco and Denise di Novi, although Denise can only really draw horses, and then only from the left-hand side. But they all had displays with good drawings. (Even if Denise's minke whales did look like horses from the left-hand side.)

Larry Franco's group had some good drawings of narwhals. You know, those weird underwater unicorn-type things with a big spike sticking out of their noses, but they didn't have any maps and the written stuff didn't look as good as ours.

Across from us, Andy Melniker had pinned up this really brilliant drawing of a whaling scene. A sperm whale was heaving up out of a stormy sea, and a bunch of guys in this little rowing boat were being tipped every which way in all this white foam.

'That's a great picture,' I told him.

'Thanks,' he said. 'Who did your drawings?'

'Stacy did,' Pippa said.

'Neat!' Andy said. 'My uncle helped me with mine.'

'My sister helped me with ours,' I said.

'But we did all the written stuff ourselves,' Pippa said.

'And the map,' Fern said.

We heard Ms Fenwick calling for us to meet up by the main entrance.

'I'm very impressed with all your hard work,' she said once she'd quietened us down.

'Nat Pederson will be here in half an hour. I want you all back here by your displays at that time.'

'I'm going to check whether my folks have arrived yet,' I told the others once Ms Fenwick had dismissed us. 'See you in a few minutes.'

I went through the swinging doors and up the steps that led to the main pool. There were plenty of people wandering around. Kids from our school and a whole load of kids that I didn't know from other schools, as well as a few parents. (It wasn't really a *parents* thing, but a few had come along to watch.)

I found Amanda and her cheerleading squad in a huddle in one corner of the girls' locker room. She was doing some last-minute coaching for their new cheer. They were all in their cheerleading outfits and looking pretty nervous.

'Natalie,' I heard Amanda say. 'I've been over this twenty million times with you.'

Natalie was standing there with this dumb expression on her face. (And Natalie's dumb expressions take some beating.)

'I've got it,' Natalie said. 'I don't know what you're worrying about.'

'I'm worrying about you jumping to the right when everyone else is jumping to the *left*!'

Amanda said. 'That's what I'm worrying about.'

'Hi!' I said.

Amanda glared at me. 'Beat it,' she snapped.

'Oh, charming,' I said. 'I only came by to wish you luck.'

'There's no *luck* involved,' Amanda said angrily. 'If everyone knows what they're supposed to be doing here, we won't *need* any luck.' She stared meaningfully at Natalie. Natalie just blinked at her as if she didn't know what Amanda meant.

'I've obviously picked a bad time,' I said, backing out. Phew! So much for the new nicer Amanda.

I stuck my head around the door again. 'Hey! Break a leg!' I said.

'Wha-at?' Amanda yelled.

'That's what you're supposed to say to people who are about to perform,' I said. 'Break a leg!'

'Get OUT!' Amanda hollered.

'OK,' I said. 'I can take a hint.'

I found Mom and Dad up in the spectators' gallery with some other parents.

'Are you going to come and look at our display?' I asked.

'We sure are,' Dad said. 'Right after the show.'

I sat with them for a few minutes. From up there you could see the sunlight sparkling on the water in the pool through the glass roof. At the far end were the diving boards and a table set up for the judges.

'Have you seen Amanda anywhere?' Mom asked.

'She's in the locker room,' I told her. 'Yelling at everyone.'

'I imagine she's pretty nervous,' Dad said. 'They'll do fine.'

'Everyone likes my drawings,' I said. 'I'm sure glad I got Amanda to help.'

Mom and Dad gave each other a knowing look.

'And what about that book report?' Mom said.

'How did you *know* I was doing the report for her?' I asked.

'Moms just do,' Mom said mysteriously. 'It wasn't too hard to figure out, Stacy. You had to be doing *something* for her to make up for all the running around you had her doing.'

'She's not going to use the report I did,' I said. 'But once she's finished reading the book, I'm going to help her with her own report.' I looked hopefully at them. 'That's OK, isn't it?'

Mom gave me a hug. 'That's just how it should be,' she said. 'I'm really pleased with both of you.'

You see? I told you Mom is always in a good mood when Dad gets home. It's a real shame he can't be here *all* the time.

★ ★ ★

I went back down to the foyer and met up with my friends. Nat Pederson was due any minute and everyone was getting real excited.

We all gave him a big cheer when he arrived. And, you know, he was like a real, normal guy. He wasn't at all like you'd imagine a famous person to be. I'd only ever seen photos of him, and it wasn't until I saw him up close that I realized how big he was. And was he good-looking? Wow! When he finishes with high-diving he'd make a perfect action hero in the movies.

Ms Fenwick showed him all around the exhibition and he kept stopping to ask questions and say nice things. He spent a couple of minutes talking to the four of us about our stuff and telling us what a good job we'd done, while Ms Fenwick stood in the background with this big smile on her face.

Then it was time for us all to go into the spectators' galleries in the main pool.

I cheered like mad when Amanda and the gang did their special Nat Pederson cheer. It went perfectly. Even Natalie seemed to have finally got the hang of it.

And then Nat did some spectacular dives off the high board and we all applauded like crazy.

Once he'd finished his display the swim meet got going and we all did a lot more cheering and shouting. By the end of the meet I was almost hoarse with all the yelling I'd been doing. When all the points were totalled up, Four Corners Middle School had won by *four* points! Way to GO!

Chapter Fifteen

'The cafeteria is opening late today,' Ms Fenwick told us on the bus back to school. 'So you can all go straight there for your lunch. Afternoon classes will be starting an hour later than usual.'

'Does that mean we have to stay an extra hour to make up time?' Fern called.

'No,' Ms Fenwick said. 'You'll go home at the normal time.'

There was a big cheer.

Everyone was still really excited after the swim meet. And missing an hour of school didn't exactly depress anyone, either.

But there was one thing still on my mind. After the competition had finished, Mom and Dad had looked around the exhibition. Amanda had been there too, looking very pleased with herself.

I had been standing by our display, basking in Mom and Dad's praise when Amanda had put her mouth up close to my ear.

'Your chores start as soon as we get back to school,' she had hissed. 'Waitress service in the cafeteria.'

Mom would call this: 'chickens coming home to roost'. I'd made Amanda look small in front of her friends, and now she was about to do the same for me.

Of course, I could always not go to the cafeteria at all. But I had promised to make up for all the chores Amanda had done for me. I couldn't go back on my promise.

I was just walking to the cafeteria with my friends when I had this idea.

'I've got things to do,' I said to the others. 'I'll see you up there.'

'What things?' Cindy asked.

'You'll see,' I called as I ran back down the stairs. I went down to the main office. There was a small table and a few chairs set up for visitors outside the school secretary's office. There were always magazines on the table, and a vase of flowers, to make the place look cheerful.

I grabbed the vase and headed full speed for the school nurse's office. There was no one there. I went in and took a folded sheet out of the cabinet. As long as no one stopped me and asked what I thought I was doing, this was going to work perfectly.

150

Amanda wanted waitress service. She was going to get waitress service *plus*!

I made a quick stop off at my locker to pick up a notebook, then ran to the cafeteria. There was a really long line waiting to be served, but plenty of tables were still unoccupied.

'Stacy Allen, what are you doing?' Ms Guber asked as I ran in. Ms Guber was on lunch patrol.

'Fixing up a special table for the head cheer-leader,' I said. 'She deserves it for working out that new cheer.'

Ms Guber gave me a puzzled look for a second, and then smiled.

'Go right ahead,' she said.

Plenty of heads turned as I spread the sheet out on one of the tables and planted the vase of flowers in the middle.

I looked around at the line. Amanda and a few of her pals were about halfway down.

'Reserved table for Amanda Allen and friends,' I yelled above the noise. 'Take your seats, please.' Amanda and her friends looked at one another, then Amanda came out of the line.

'What are you talking about?' she said, giving me a suspicious look. 'Is this some kind of joke?'

'No joke,' I said. 'You wanted waitress

service? You've got it.' I pulled a chair out for her. 'Would madam care to sit here?'

Amanda grinned and called the other three Cheer-Bimbos over. They all sat down and I got out my notebook.

'Are you ready to order?' I asked, trying to sound like a waitress at a five-star restaurant. 'I can particularly recommend the meatloaf today.'

Amanda laughed. 'Stacy,' she said. 'You're *some* kind of nut!'

Everyone was looking at us and there were a lot of calls of: 'Hey, waitress, my table next!' and plenty of laughing. But the great thing was that they weren't laughing *at* me. I'd come up with a way of giving Amanda and her pals waitress service without making myself look like I was being humiliated.

And that takes brains.

*   *   *

I got home feeling really pleased with myself. And the nicest thing of all was that Dad was there. He was in the kitchen, making hamburgers from a secret recipe that he says has been passed down through his family for generations.

The back door was open and I could see the barbecue had been set up.

'Barbecue!' I yelled. 'Great!'

He looked at me. He was wearing an apron with *HEAD COOK* written on it.

'Hello, sweetheart,' he said. 'I think your mom would like a word with you. She's in the basement.'

Uh-oh. *Now* what?

I went down the stairs. Mom was sitting at her desk, typing stuff into her word processor. The doors to the big closet down there were open and there was a huge pile of junk scattered over the floor.

She looked at me. 'When I ask you to clean up the basement,' she said. 'I don't mean for you to shove everything in the closet any old way and then slam the door on it.'

'Oh. Well, yes, but . . .' I nearly said *but Amanda did it*, except that I didn't think Mom would go for that as a reasonable excuse. Not when she'd specifically asked me to clean up down there for her.

She nodded toward the mess of stuff on the floor. I could see what had happened. Typical Amanda! She'd just crammed the closet tight and locked the door. Mom had opened the closet and everything had come tumbling out.

'How about you do the job properly?' she said. 'Like, *now*!'

'Yes, ma'am,' I said.

'And I want it so the stuff doesn't fall out on me when I open the door,' Mom said.

I started picking the stuff up off the floor.

I heard a yell down the stairs. It was Amanda.

'Hey, Stacy! You down there?'

'Yes,' I called back.

'I've got that *list* for you,' she shouted. 'When you're ready to start.' The list? Oh, right! The list of chores.

You know, it's kind of strange. No matter how things work out between Amanda and me, *somehow* I always end up having to clear up after her.

My sister the slave? I don't think so. If there's a slave in this house her name's Stacy Allen, and you'd better believe it!

LITTLE SISTER
Book 3

Preview

Stacy and Amanda are back in **Little Sister Book 3**, *Stacy the Matchmaker*, coming soon from Red Fox. Here's a sneak preview:

Chapter One

Crash!

'Eyyow!' I yelled. It wasn't the noise of my sister Amanda slamming her bedroom door that made me yell, it was Benjamin, my cat. One second he was fast asleep on my legs and the next there was this flurry of scrabbling claws and paws as he zipped under my bed.

My sister Amanda often has that effect. There are times when I feel like hiding under the bed myself to get away from Amanda. Especially when she's in one of her moods. And judging by the way she'd just slammed her bedroom door, she was in a hurricane-alert, head-for-the-bomb-shelters, women-children-and-cats-first, mega-bad mood.

Bang!

That was Amanda's closet door. Her bedroom's right next to mine, so I get to hear all about it when Amanda's on the rampage.

I'd only been home from school for half an hour and I *had* been lying peacefully on my bed with Benjamin dozing on my legs while I read a book.

Now I tipped myself over the edge of the bed and peered underneath. Benjamin stared out at me from the gloom.

'It's OK,' I told him. 'She's not after you. You're perfectly safe.' I reached under the bed to give him a reassuring stroke.

Whack!

It sounded like she was kicking the furniture. Amanda only kicks the furniture when something *really* bad has happened. Like discovering a big red zit sitting on the end of her nose.

'I'd better go and check what the problem is,' I told Benjamin, as I climbed off my bed. 'Before she demolishes the whole house.'

I went along the hall and listened at Amanda's bedroom door.

Thud! I heard from inside. And then, 'Ow!'

'You OK in there?' I called.

'Ow! No!' Amanda yelled.

I opened the door and peeked in. Amanda was sitting on the bed clutching her foot. She scowled at me.

'What do you want, Stacy?' she said, rubbing her toes.

'Oh, it's only you,' I said with a grin. 'I

thought a mad gorilla was on the loose in here.' I gave her a friendly smile.

'The only monkey around here is *you*!' Amanda snapped.

'Gorillas aren't monkeys,' I said. 'Gorillas are apes. I read it in a book. All monkeys have tails, but gorillas – '

'I don't care!' yelled Amanda.

'Tell me to mind my own business, if you like,' I said, 'but is something upsetting you?'

'I've hurt my foot,' Amanda said.

'That's what happens when you kick the furniture,' I told her.

'Who asked you?'

'You're in a bad mood,' I said. 'I can tell.'

'Get lost!'

'Don't take it out on me,' I said. 'I'm only trying to be helpful. What happened?'

Amanda glared at me. 'Nothing happened. I can kick the furniture if I like. It's my furniture. I don't need permission from you before I can kick my own furniture.'

'Are you in trouble at school?' I asked.

This seemed the most likely explanation. Amanda is always getting into trouble with her teachers for forgetting homework and stuff like that. The only things Amanda really likes about school are gossiping with her friends and being head cheerleader. The rest kind of passes her by.

'School? Huh!' Amanda said.

'Have you got a zit?'

'Get out of here!'

So it wasn't zits and it wasn't school. But something had happened. Even Amanda doesn't kick furniture for fun.

'Tell me,' I said. 'Maybe I can help?'

'Oh, sure,' Amanda said. 'I guess there's a whole bunch of stuff you can do to help me with *her*!'

Ha! Now we were getting somewhere. There was a "her" involved.

'Did Cheryl say something?' I asked. Cheryl Ruddick was one of Amanda's Bimbo friends. I don't like Cheryl very much. If she was my friend she'd be annoying me all the time. Not that an air-head like Cheryl Ruddick would ever *be* my friend.

Amanda stared at me. 'What's Cheryl got to do with anything?' she asked.

'How should I know?' I said. 'You said *her*. I thought maybe – '

'I'm talking about Judy MacWilliams,' Amanda yelled.

Of course! Judy MacWilliams.

Amanda's hate list goes something like this: 1. *School Work*, 2. *Chores around the house*, and

3. *Judy MacWilliams*. (I'm usually somewhere in Amanda's top ten hates, the same way she's usually in mine – but right then neither of us were at number one).

Amanda and Judy are, like, total rivals in their class. At this point I have to say that Amanda's kind of pretty – if you like blue-eyed bimbos with wavy blonde hair. Judy is pretty, too, with long glossy black hair and Barbie doll looks. If our school held a Vanity Competition, I'm not sure who'd come top out of Judy and Amanda. But it would be *one* of them, that's for sure.

Amanda's last great triumph over Judy had been when Judy ended up with plaster of Paris all over her at Amanda's thirteenth birthday party, and had left the house in disgrace. (I haven't got time to explain how that happened right now, but it was a riot). I hadn't heard much from Amanda about Judy since then, but judging by the expression on Amanda's face just then, Judy MacWilliams was right up there at the top of Amanda's hate list again.

'What did she do?' I asked. It made a nice change for Amanda to be ticked off with someone other than me. I was dying to know what had happened.

'Nothing!' Amanda snapped.

'Nothing?' I said. 'She's got you this mad

by doing *nothing*?' Sheesh – what was it going to be like when Judy did *something*?

'She's just acting so *big*,' said Amanda. 'She thinks she's so smart. As if I care!' Amanda got up off the bed and stamped around the room. 'I don't care!' she yelled. 'I don't care *at all*!'

'Hey!' came Mom's voice up the stairs. 'What's all the noise? Are you two fighting again? I can hear you all the way down in the basement.'

I ran out of Amanda's room and hung over the banisters.

'We're not fighting,' I called. 'Amanda's in a bad mood because of Judy MacWilliams. Even though Judy MacWilliams hasn't done anything, and Amanda says she doesn't care, anyway.'

'I don't!' Amanda yelled, slamming the door behind me.

'Stacy, tell Amanda to keep the noise down,' Mom called. 'If she wakes Sam up I'll make sure she *does* care, right?'

'Mom?' I called softly.

'Yes?'

'You'll wake Sam up.'

Mom gave one of her growly 'Hmmms'.

I heard Amanda locking her door. Rats! She'd locked herself in there. Now how was I going to find out what Judy MacWilliams had done?

I went back to my room. Still no sign of Benjamin.

I lay on the floor and peered under the bed. He was all the way at the back. I could see his eyes staring at me.

'Come on out, you big coward,' I told him.

He came slinking out and rubbed himself along my face, purring up a storm, his grey fur tickling my nose.

I sneezed. 'Look at you!' I said. 'All covered in dust.' I lifted him into my arms. 'You need a good brushing.'

Benjamin likes it when I brush him. I've got a special fine-toothed comb for him. I did his back, and then he rolled over like a big softie so I could comb his tummy.

'Our sister is in a bad mood,' I told him. 'And it's something to do with Judy MacWilliams.' Brush, brush. 'Amanda wouldn't tell me what it's all about. So you know what I'm going to do?' He stretched his chin out so I could carefully comb his neck.

'I'll tell you,' I said. 'Tomorrow at school, I'm going to find our for myself what that nasty Judy MacWilliams has done.' I combed behind his ears. 'What do your think of *that*?'

I guessed from the volume of Benjamin's

purrs that he agreed with me. After all, Amanda is my *sister*, even if she does drive me nuts at times. And when someone has upset my sister, it's my *duty* to try and put things right if I can.

* * *

It was time to go home and I was having a last chat with my friends in front of the school. I'd told the guys about Amanda's bad mood the previous afternoon.

'Judy's probably showing off with some flashy new clothes,' Cindy said.

'It's got to be something bigger than that,' I said. 'Something that would really drive Amanda wild. You should have heard her.'

'Hey,' Fern said. 'I think I might have the answer. Look!' She pointed out through the gates.

There were plenty of people standing around chatting, but you couldn't miss Judy. For a start she had her horrible sidekick with her, Maddie Fischer. Maddie is kind of creepy. She trails about after Judy like a pet dog. No, that's not fair. I like dogs. Maddie is more like a swamp-monster.

But it wasn't Maddie that caught our attention.

It was the boy that Judy was talking to that

we all looked at. He looked about fifteen, and even from that distance you could see the way Judy was showing off in front of him. I'll be honest with you, and say that he was kind of cute, if you like boys. He had blonde hair and a big denim jacket covered in buttons. There are quite a few boys like that around Four Corners, all looking like they think they're movie stars or something. But we didn't often see any of them hanging around in front of our school.

'Who is he?' Pippa asked.

'I don't know,' I said. 'I don't think I've ever seen him before.'

'He must be from the high school,' Cindy said.

'So what's he doing around here?' Pippa said.

Fern gave her a knowing look. 'What does it look like he's doing?' she said. 'He's here to see Judy.'

'Wow!' Pippa said. 'You mean – '

'Look!' Fern interrupted. 'He's taking her bag. And he's got his arm around her. They're *kissing*!'

They were, too. Right there in front of everyone.

We watched as Judy and the boy finished kissing and walked off. Maddie trotted after them for a few paces, then Judy looked around at her and said something. Maddie came to a halt, her shoulders sort of *sagging*. Judy and the boy walked together along the pavement. Maddie stood looking after them for a few moments then wandered off on her own.

'Judy has a boyfriend,' I said, as the light dawned on me. 'That's what Amanda is so mad about! Judy MacWilliams has gotten herself a boyfriend!'

Other great reads from Red Fox

Little Sister Series by Allan Frewin Jones

LITTLE SISTER 1 – THE GREAT SISTER WAR

Meet Stacy Allen of Four Corners Indiana. She's your average ten year old – a brown-haired, skinny tomboy and a bit of a bookworm. *Now* meet her sister, Amanda, aged 13 and a fully-fledged teenager. She's an all-American, blue-eyed blonde and she's too busy being a cool cheerleader and a trendy *artiste* to want a little sister hanging around. Stacy thinks Amanda and her friends are total airheads and Amanda calls Stacy's gang nerds; they have the biggest love-hate relationship of the century and that can only mean one thing – The Great Sister War.
ISBN 0 09 938381 0   £2.99

LITTLE SISTER 2 – MY SISTER, MY SLAVE

Stacy and Amanda, the arch rivals in sisterhood, are back with a vengeance! When Amanda, cheerleader extra-ordinaire, starts to become a school slacker Mom is ready to take drastic action – pull Amanda out of the cheerleading squad! So the sisters make a deal: Stacy agrees to write Amanda's school report in return for two days of slavery. What Amanda doesn't realize is that when her little sister's boss, two days means 48 *whole* hours of chores – snea-kee!
ISBN 0 09 938391 8   £2.99

Other great reads from **Red Fox**

Little Sister Series by Allan Frewin Jones

LITTLE SISTER 1 – THE GREAT SISTER WAR

Meet Stacy Allen, a ten year old tomboy and a bit of a bookworm. *Now* meet her blue-eyed blonde sister, Amanda, just turned 13 and a fully-fledged teenager. Stacy thinks Amanda's a total airhead and Amanda calls Stacy and her gang the nerds; they have the biggest love-hate relationship of the century and that can only mean one thing – war.
ISBN 0 09 938381 0   £2.99

LITTLE SISTER 2 – MY SISTER, MY SLAVE

When Amanda starts to become a school slacker, Mom is ready to take drastic action – pull Amanda out of the cheerleading squad! So the sisters make a deal; Stacy will help Amanda with her school work in return for two whole days of slavery. But Amanda doesn't realize that when her little sister's boss, two days means 48 *whole* hours of chores – snea-kee!
ISBN 0 09 938391 8   £2.99

LITTLE SISTER 3 – STACY THE MATCHMAKER

Amanda is mad that the school Barbie doll, Judy McWilliams, has got herself a boyfriend, and to make things worse it's hunky Greg Masterson, the guy Amanda has fancied for ages. Stacy feels that it's her duty as sister to fix Amanda's lovelife and decides to play cupid and do a bit of matchmaking, with disastrous results!
ISBN 0 09 938401 9   £2.99

LITTLE SISTER 4 – COPYCAT

Cousin Laine is so coo-ol! She's a glamorous 18 year old and wears gorgeous clothes, and has got a boyfriend with a car. When Stacy and Amanda's parents go away for a week leaving Laine in charge, 13 year old Amanda decides she wants to be just like her cousin and begins to copy Laine's every move . . .
ISBN 0 09 938411 6   £2.99

Other great reads from **Red Fox**

Further Red Fox titles that you might enjoy reading are listed on the following pages. They are available in bookshops or they can be ordered directly from us.

If you would like to order books, please send this form and the money due to:

ARROW BOOKS, BOOKSERVICE BY POST, PO BOX 29, DOUGLAS, ISLE OF MAN, BRITISH ISLES. Please enclose a cheque or postal order made out to Arrow Books Ltd for the amount due, plus 75p per book for postage and packing to a maximum of £7.50, both for orders within the UK. For customers outside the UK, please allow £1.00 per book.

NAME_____

ADDRESS_____

_____

Please print clearly.

Whilst every effort is made to keep prices low, it is sometimes necessary to increase cover prices at short notice. If you are ordering books by post, to save delay it is advisable to phone to confirm the correct price. The number to ring is THE SALES DEPARTMENT 071 (if outside London) 973 9700.

BESTSELLING FICTION FROM RED FOX

☐	The Present Takers	Aidan Chambers	£2.99
☐	Battle for the Park	Colin Dann	£2.99
☐	Orson Cart Comes Apart	Steve Donald	£1.99
☐	The Last Vampire	Willis Hall	£2.99
☐	Harvey Angell	Diana Hendry	£2.99
☐	Emil and the Detectives	Erich Kästner	£2.99
☐	Krindlekrax	Philip Ridley	£2.99

PRICES AND OTHER DETAILS ARE LIABLE TO CHANGE

ARROW BOOKS, BOOKSERVICE BY POST, PO BOX 29,
DOUGLAS, ISLE OF MAN, BRITISH ISLES

NAME ....

ADDRESS ....

....

....

Please enclose a cheque or postal order made out to B.S.B.P. Ltd. for
the amount due and allow the following for postage and packing:

U.K. CUSTOMERS: Please allow 75p per book to a maximum of
£7.50

B.F.P.O. & EIRE: Please allow 75p per book to a maximum of £7.50

OVERSEAS CUSTOMERS: Please allow £1.00 per book.

While every effort is made to keep prices low it is sometimes necessary
to increase cover prices at short notice. Arrow Books reserve the right
to show new retail prices on covers which may differ from those
previously advertised in the text or elsewhere.

BESTSELLING FICTION FROM RED FOX

☐	The Story of Doctor Dolittle	Hugh Lofting	£3.99
☐	Amazon Adventure	Willard Price	£3.99
☐	Swallows and Amazons	Arthur Ransome	£3.99
☐	The Wolves of Willoughby Chase	Joan Aiken	£2.99
☐	Steps up the Chimney	William Corlett	£2.99
☐	The Snow-Walker's Son	Catherine Fisher	£2.99
☐	Redwall	Brian Jacques	£3.99
☐	Guilty!	Ruth Thomas	£2.99

PRICES AND OTHER DETAILS ARE LIABLE TO CHANGE

ARROW BOOKS, BOOKSERVICE BY POST, PO BOX 29, DOUGLAS, ISLE OF MAN, BRITISH ISLES

NAME ....

ADDRESS ....

....

....

Please enclose a cheque or postal order made out to B.S.B.P. Ltd. for the amount due and allow the following for postage and packing:

U.K. CUSTOMERS: Please allow 75p per book to a maximum of £7.50

B.F.P.O. & EIRE: Please allow 75p per book to a maximum of £7.50

OVERSEAS CUSTOMERS: Please allow £1.00 per book.

While every effort is made to keep prices low it is sometimes necessary to increase cover prices at short notice. Arrow Books reserve the right to show new retail prices on covers which may differ from those previously advertised in the text or elsewhere.

BESTSELLING FICTION FROM RED FOX

☐ Blood	Alan Durant	£3.50
☐ Tina Come Home	Paul Geraghty	£3.50
☐ Del-Del	Victor Kelleher	£3.50
☐ Paul Loves Amy Loves Christo	Josephine Poole	£3.50
☐ If It Weren't for Sebastian	Jean Ure	£3.50
☐ You'll Never Guess the End	Barbara Wersba	£3.50
☐ The Pigman	Paul Zindel	£3.50

PRICES AND OTHER DETAILS ARE LIABLE TO CHANGE

ARROW BOOKS, BOOKSERVICE BY POST, PO BOX 29,
DOUGLAS, ISLE OF MAN, BRITISH ISLES

NAME...

ADDRESS...

....

....

Please enclose a cheque or postal order made out to B.S.B.P. Ltd. for
the amount due and allow the following for postage and packing:

U.K. CUSTOMERS: Please allow 75p per book to a maximum of
£7.50

B.F.P.O. & EIRE: Please allow 75p per book to a maximum of £7.50

OVERSEAS CUSTOMERS: Please allow £1.00 per book.

While every effort is made to keep prices low it is sometimes necessary
to increase cover prices at short notice. Arrow Books reserve the right
to show new retail prices on covers which may differ from those
previously advertised in the text or elsewhere.

Top teenage fiction from Red Fox

PLAY NIMROD FOR HIM   Jean Ure

Christopher and Nick are each other's only friend. Isolated from the rest of the crowd, they live in their own world of writing and music. Enter lively, popular Sal who tempts Christopher away from Nick . . .
ISBN 0 09 985300 0   £2.99

HAMLET, BANANAS AND ALL THAT JAZZ
Alan Durant

Bert, Jim and their mates vow to live dangerously – just as Nietzsche said. So starts a post-GCSEs summer of girls, parties, jazz, drink, fags . . . and tragedy.
ISBN 0 09 997540 8   £3.50

ENOUGH IS TOO MUCH ALREADY
Jan Mark

Maurice, Nina and Nazzer are all re-sitting their O levels but prefer to spend their time musing over hilarious previous encounters with strangers, hamsters, wild parties and Japanese radishes . . .
ISBN 0 09 985310 8   £2.99

BAD PENNY   Allan Frewin Jones

Christmas doesn't look good for Penny this year. She's veggy, feels overweight, *and* The Lizard, her horrible father has just turned up. Worse still, Roy appears – Penny's ex whom she took a year to get over.
ISBN 0 09 985280 2   £2.99

CUTTING LOOSE   Carole Lloyd

Charlie's horoscope says to get back into the swing of things, but it's not easy: her Dad and Gran aren't speaking, she's just found out the truth about her mum, and is having severe confused spells about her lovelife. It's time to cut loose from all binding ties, and decide what she wants and who she really is.
ISBN 0 09 91381 X   £3.50

Other great reads *from* **Red Fox**

Teenage thrillers from Red Fox

GOING TO EGYPT   Helen Dunmore

When Dad announces they're going on holiday to
Weston, Colette is disappointed – she'd much rather
be going to Egypt. But when she meets the boys who
ride their horses in the sea at dawn, she realizes that
it isn't where you go that counts, it's who you meet
while you're there . . .
ISBN 0 09 910901 8   £3.50

BLOOD   Alan Durant

Life turns frighteningly upside down when Robert hears
his parents have been shot dead in the family home. The
police, the psychiatrists, the questions . . . Robert
decides to carry out his own investigations, and pushes
his sanity to the brink.
ISBN 0 09 992330 0   £3.50

DEL-DEL   Victor Kelleher

Des, Hannah and their children are a close-knit family
– or so it seems. But suddenly, a year after the death
of their daughter Laura, Sam the youngest son starts
to act very strangely – having been possessed by a
terrifyingly evil presence called Del-Del.
ISBN 0 09 918271 8   £3.50

THE GRANITE BEAST   Ann Coburn

After her father's death, Ruth is uprooted from town-
life to a close-knit Cornish village and feels lost and
alone. But the strange and terrifying dreams she has
every night are surely from something more than just
unhappiness? Only Ben, another outsider, seems to
understand the omen of major disaster . . .
ISBN 0 09 985970 X   £2.99

Sigh and swoon with our romantic reads

IF IT WEREN'T FOR SEBASTIAN   Jean Ure

Sensible Maggie's family are shocked when she moves into a bedsit to learn shorthand and typing. Maggie herself is shocked when she meets enigmatic, eccentric Sebastian – the unlikeliest of housemates. But a cat called Sunday brings them together – then almost tears them apart . . .
ISBN 0 09 985870 3   £3.50

I NEVER LOVED YOUR MIND   Paul Zindel

Dewey Daniels and Yvette Goethals seem the unlikeliest of couples – he thinks she's an adolescent ghoul, and she despises him for being a carnivore. Yet despite himself, Dewey finds himself falling in love with her – which leads to utter disaster!
ISBN 0 09 987270 6   £3.50

SEVEN WEEKS LAST SUMMER
Catherine Robinson

Abby's only plans that summer were to catch up on her revision for the mock exams and enjoy the sun. Instead, the summer becomes a time of change for Abby, her family and her friends, too.
ISBN 0 09 918551 2   £3.50

I CAPTURE THE CASTLE   Dodie Smith

In this wonderfully romantic book, Cassandra Mortmain tells the story of the changes in the life of her extraordinary and impoverished family after the arrival of their rich and handsome young American landlord.
ISBN 0 09 984500 8   £3.99

Join the RED FOX Reader's Club

The Red Fox Reader's Club is for readers of all ages. All you have to do is ask your local bookseller or librarian for a Red Fox Reader's Club card. As an official Red Fox Reader you only have to borrow or buy eight Red Fox books in order to qualify for your own Red Fox Reader's Clubpack – full of exciting surprises! If you have any difficulty obtaining a Red Fox Reader's Club card please write to: Random House Children's Books Marketing Department, 20 Vauxhall Bridge Road, London SW1V 2SA.